RANDOM HOUSE

LARGE PRINT

# Death in
# Her Hands

ALSO BY OTTESSA MOSHFEGH
AVAILABLE FROM RANDOM
HOUSE LARGE PRINT

**My Year of Rest and Relaxation**

# Death in

# Her Hands

## Ottessa Moshfegh

R A N D O M   H O U S E
**LARGE PRINT**

Copyright © 2020 by Ottessa Moshfegh

Published in the United States of America by
Random House Large Print
in association with Penguin Press,
an imprint of Penguin Random House LLC.

Cover design and illustration: Oliver Munday

The Library of Congress has established a
Cataloging-in-Publication record for this title.

ISBN: 978-0-593-17190-5

www.penguinrandomhouse.com/large-print-format-books

FIRST LARGE PRINT EDITION

Printed in the United States of America
10  9  8  7  6  5  4  3  2  1

This Large Print edition published in accord with
the standards of the N.A.V.H.

# Death in
# Her Hands

## One

**Her name was Magda. Nobody will ever know who killed her. It wasn't me. Here is her dead body.**

But there was no body. No bloodstain. No tangle of hair caught on the coarse fallen branches, no red wool scarf damp with morning dew festooned across the bushes. There was just the note on the ground, rustling at my feet in the soft May wind. I happened upon it on my dawn walk through the birch woods with my dog, Charlie.

I'd discovered the path the previous spring just after Charlie and I had moved to Levant. We'd worn it down all spring, summer, and fall, but abandoned it during winter. The slim white trees had been nearly invisible against the snow. On foggy mornings, the birches completely disappeared in the mist. Since the thaw, Charlie had been waking me up every morning at daybreak. We'd cross the dirt road and trudge up the slow rise and fall of a little hill, and weave our way back and forth through the birches. That morning, when I found the note laid flat on the path, we'd made it about a mile into the woods.

Charlie did not slow or tilt his head or even lower his nose to the ground to sniff. It seemed very odd to me that he'd just ignore it—my Charlie, who once broke off his leash and ran across the freeway to fetch a dead bird, so strong was his instinct to ferret out the dead. No, he didn't give the note a second glance. Little black rocks pinned the note down to the ground, each placed carefully on the page in the top margin and along the bottom. I bent down to read it again. Under my hands, the earth was almost warm, shy pale grass poking up here and there in the crumbly black dirt, the sun just starting to brighten in hue from silver to yellow.

**Her name was Magda.**

It was a joke, I thought, a prank, a ruse. Somebody was playing games. That was my initial impression. Isn't it sweet to look back at how my mind jumped to the most innocuous conclusion? That after so many years, at seventy-two, my imagination was still so naive? Experience should have taught me that first impressions are often misleading. Kneeling down in the dirt, I considered the details: the paper was a page from a lined, spiral notebook, its perforated edge broken cleanly, no straggly bits from where it had been torn out; careful, small printed letters in blue ballpoint pen. It was hard to decipher much from the penmanship, and that seemed deliberate. It was the kind of neat, impersonal printing you'd use when making a sign for a yard sale, or filling out a form at the dentist. Wise, I thought. Smart. Whoever had written the note understood that by masking one's peculiarities, one invokes authority. There is nothing as imposing as anonymity. But the words themselves, when I spoke them aloud, seemed witty, a rare quality in Levant, where most people were blue collar and dull. I read the note again and almost chuckled over that penultimate line, **It wasn't me.** Of course it wasn't.

If not a prank, the note could have been the beginning of a story tossed out as a false start, a bad opening. I could understand the hesitation. It's a rather dark, damning way to begin a story: the pronouncement of a mystery whose investigation is futile. **Nobody will ever know who killed her.** The story is over just as it's begun. Was futility a subject worthy of exploration? The note certainly didn't promise any happy ending.

**Here is her dead body.** Surely there was more to say. Where **was** Magda? Was it so hard to come up with a description of her corpse, tangled in the brush under a fallen tree, her face half sunken into the soft black dirt, her hands hog-tied behind her back, the blood from her stab wounds leaching into the ground? How hard was it to imagine a small golden locket glinting

between sodden birch leaves, the chain
broken and dashed through the new, tender, hairy grass? The locket could contain
photos of a young, gap-toothed child on
one side—Magda at age five—and a man
in a military hat on the other, her father,
I'd guess. Or maybe "hog-tied" would be a
bit too strong. Maybe "stab wounds" were
too graphic too soon. Perhaps the killer
simply positioned her arms behind her
back so they wouldn't stick out from under
the rotting branches and catch somebody's
eye. The pale skin of Magda's hands would
stand out against the dark ground, like
the white paper on the path, I imagined.
It seemed better to begin with gentler de-
scriptions. I could write the book myself
if I had the discipline, if I thought anyone
might read it.

As I stood, my thoughts were bleached
and stunted by a terrible pain in my head
and eyes, which often happened when I got
up too quickly. I always had poor circula-
tion, low blood pressure, "a weak heart,"
my husband had called it. Or perhaps I was
hungry. I have to be careful, I told myself.

One day I might faint in the wrong place and hit my head, or cause an accident in my car. That would be the end of me. I had no one to tend to me if I fell ill. I'd die in some cheap country hospital and Charlie would get slaughtered at the pound.

Charlie, as though he could sense my dizziness, came to my side and licked my hand. In doing so, he stepped on the note. I heard the paper crinkle. Pity to have that pristine page now sullied with a paw print. But I didn't chide him. I scratched his silky head with my fingers.

Maybe I was being too imaginative, I thought, scanning the note again. I could picture a high school boy wandering the woods, thinking up some funny gore, writing these first few lines, then losing steam, discarding the story for one he found easier to conjure up: the tale of a lost sock, a fight on the football field, a man going fishing, kissing a girl behind the garage. What did some Levant teen need with Magda and her mystery? Magda. This was not a Jenny or Sally or Mary or Sue. Magda was a name for a character with substance, a mysterious past. Exotic, even. And who would want to read about that here, in Levant? The only books at Goodwill were about knitting and World War II.

"Magda. She's strange," they'd say.

"I wouldn't want Jenny or Sally to be hanging around a girl like Magda. Who knows what kind of values she was raised with?"

"Magda. What kind of name is that? An immigrant? Some different language?"

No wonder he had given up on Magda so quickly. Her situation was too complex, too nuanced for a young kid to understand. It would take a wise mind to do Magda's story real justice. Death was hard to look at, after all. "Skip it," I can imagine the boy saying, discarding these first few lines. And with that, Magda and all her potential were abandoned. However, there were no signs of neglect, or frustration, nothing revised or rewritten. On the contrary, the lines were pristine and even. Nothing was scribbled out. The paper hadn't been crumpled up or even folded. And those little rocks . . .

"Magda?" I said aloud, not knowing exactly why. Charlie seemed not to care. He busied himself chasing drifting dandelion puffs through the trees. I paced up and down the path for a few minutes, scrutinized the dirt for anything that seemed out of place, then walked around the surrounding area in a narrowing gyre. I was hoping to find another note, another clue. I whistled to Charlie every time he strayed too far. There weren't any strange new paths through the trees that I could see, but then, of course, my own shuffling around made a mess of things and confused me. Still, there was nothing. I found nothing. Not even a cigarette butt or a crushed soda can.

We'd had a TV set back in Monlith. I'd seen plenty of murder mystery shows. I could picture twin gutters etched into the dirt by the heels of a corpse being dragged. Or an impression in the ground where a body had been laid, the grass matted down, tender seedlings bent, a mushroom crushed. And then, of course, fresh black dirt covering a new, shallow grave. But the ground of the birch woods was undisturbed as far as

I could tell. Everything was as it had been the previous morning, at least in that little area. It would take days, weeks, to cover the entire woods. Poor Magda, wherever she is, I thought, turning around slowly in case I'd missed something poking out— a shoe, a plastic barrette. The note on the path seemed to indicate that she was nearby, didn't it? Wasn't the note more of a headstone than a made-up story? **Here lies Magda,** it seemed to say. What's the use of such a note, like a tag, a title, if the thing it's referring to isn't anywhere near it? Or anywhere at all, for that matter? The land was held in public trust, I knew, so anybody had the right to come through it.

Levant wasn't a particularly beautiful place. There were no covered bridges or colonial manors, no museums or historic municipal buildings. But the nature in Levant was pretty enough to distinguish it from Bethsmane, the neighboring township. We were two hours from the coast. A big river ran through Bethsmane, and people would sail through up from Maconsett in summer, I'd heard. So the area wasn't completely ignored by the world outside of it. Still, it wasn't any kind of destination. There were no sights to see in Bethsmane. Main Street was boarded up. It had once been a mill town with brick sidewalks and old warehouses that, if they still existed, would have made for a charming old town. But there were no ghosts or romance left there. Bethsmane now was just a strip mall, a bowling alley and bar with glaring neon, a tiny post office that closed at noon each day, a few fast-food restaurants off the freeway. Out in Levant, we didn't even have our own post office, not that I sent or received much mail. There was a gas station with a small general store that sold bait and essentials, canned food, candy, cheap beer. I had no idea what the few residents of Levant did for recreation, other than drink and go bowling in Bethsmane. They didn't strike me as the type of folks to take scenic strolls. So who, then, would have found his way into my beloved birch woods and felt the need to upset things with a note about a dead body?

"Charlie?" I called out, when I had reached the path again.

I walked back to the note, still fluttering gently in the warm wind. For a moment it seemed alive somehow, a strange and fragile creature weighed down by the black rocks, struggling to be free, like a butterfly or a bird with a broken wing. Like Magda must have felt, I imagined, under the hands of the one who killed her. Who could have done such a thing? **It wasn't me,** the note insisted. And for the first time that morning, as though it had just occurred to me to be frightened, a chill went through my bones. **Her name was Magda.** It seemed so sinister all of a sudden. It seemed so real.

Where was that dog? Waiting for Charlie to come bounding back to me through the birches, I got the feeling that I ought not lift my eyes too high, that there might be someone watching me from up in the trees. A madman in the boughs. A ghost. A god. Or Magda herself. A hungry zombie. A purgatoried soul looking for a live body to possess. When I heard Charlie thundering through the trees, I dared myself to look up. There wasn't anybody there, of course. "Be reasonable," I told myself, bracing for the head rush that I hoped courage might stave off as I knelt down to collect the little black rocks. I put them in my coat pocket and picked up the note.

If I'd been alone there in the woods, without my dog, would I have been so bold? I may have left the note there on the path and run away, rushed home to drive to the police station in Bethsmane. "There's been a murder," I might have said. What nonsense I'd describe. "I found a note in the woods. A woman named Magda. No, I didn't see her body. Just the note. I left it there, of course. But it says she's been killed. I didn't want to disturb the scene. Magda. Yes, Magda. I don't know her last name. No, I don't know her. I haven't met a Magda in all my life. I just found the note, just now. Please, hurry. Oh, please go out there right away." I would have seemed hysterical. It wasn't good for my health to get so worked up. Walter had always told me that when I got emotional, it put a great strain on my heart. "Danger zone," he'd say, and insist on putting me to bed and turning down the lights, drawing the curtains closed if it was daytime. "Best to lie down and rest until the fit passes." It was true that when I got anxious, it was hard to keep my wits about me. I got clumsy. I got dizzy. Even just walking home to the cabin in my anxiety, I could have tripped and fallen. I could have broken an arm or a hip tumbling down the little hill from the birch woods to the road. Someone could have driven by and seen me, an old lady covered in dirt, trembling with fear over what—a piece of paper? I'd have waved my arms. "Stop! There's been a murder! Magda is dead!" What a commotion I could have caused. How embarrassing that would have been.

But with Charlie around, I was calm. Nobody could say I hadn't been calm. I'd been living well the whole year in Levant, peaceful and satisfied, and pleased with my decision to make such a drastic move so many thousands of miles across the country from Monlith. I was proud that I'd had the pluck to sell the house, pack up, and leave. Truth be told, I would still be back there in that old house if it hadn't been for Charlie. I wouldn't have had the courage to move. It was comforting to have an animal, so consistently near and needy, to focus on, to nurture. Just to have another heart beating in the room, a live energy, had cheered me. I hadn't realized how lonely I'd been, and then suddenly I wasn't alone at all. I had a dog. Never again would I be alone, I thought. What a gift to have such a companion, like a child and protector, both, something wiser than me in so many ways, and yet doting, loyal, and affectionate.

The worst I'd felt since getting Charlie was that day with the dead bird back in Monlith. Charlie had never been off the leash before except at the fenced-in dog park at Lithgate Greens, and watching him run off like that across the freeway, I'd felt I was losing him forever. We'd been together just a few months then, and I was still finding my footing as his master, still a little shy, hesitant—insecure, you'd say. As I stood there, I worried that the bond between us wasn't strong enough to keep him from chasing a better life, exploring new pastures, being more of a dog than he could be with me. I was only human, after all. Wasn't I limited? Wasn't I a bore? But then I thought, what could be better than the life I had to offer him? Really, what? To run free in the hills over Monlith, to chase grouse? He'd be eaten by coyotes. And anyway, he wasn't that kind of dog. He was bred for service, to fetch, retrieve, and always to return. I'd asked myself, watching him disappear across the freeway, what I could have done to make him more comfortable, feel more important, more loved, more anything. Was he not satisfied? Was he not pampered? I could have cooked for him, I'd thought. The women at the dog park had spoken about "the toxicity of name-brand kibble." Oh, there was always more one could do to keep a creature happy. I should have made him bones, sappy with marrow, I thought, and I should have let him sleep in my bed with me. It was too cold in the kitchen of that old house in Monlith, even with the dog bed and fuzzy fleece blanket. I'd wrapped him in that blanket and held him like a newborn baby in my arms that first night in the old drafty house. He'd cried and cried, and I'd soothed him and promised him, "Nothing bad will ever happen to you. I won't let it. I love you too much. I promise, you are safe now, here, with me, forever."

And a few months later—how fast he'd grown!—I took him out for a walk and he pulled and tugged and broke loose. That morning in Monlith, his leash simply snapped and he was gone, crushing through the thin crust of snow down the hill and over the freeway.

It felt like only yesterday, I thought then, over a year later, walking home through the birches in Levant with the note, my heart beating hard. What would I have done without Charlie? How close had I come to losing him that day in Monlith? I had run after him, of course, but couldn't bring myself to step over the sharp metal guardrail that he had leapt over so effortlessly. Even at that early hour, with just a car or two passing slowly on the ice, it seemed too dangerous to step foot on the freeway blacktop. I've never been one to break any rules. It was not out of a sense of civic duty or pride or moral certitude, but it was the way I was raised. In fact, the only time I'd ever been admonished was in kindergarten. I stepped out of line on the way down to the music room, and the teacher raised her voice. "Vesta, where are you going? You think you are so special to wander off alone like a queen?" I never forgave myself. And my mother was very keen on discipline. I was never beaten or restrained. But there was always order, and when I behaved as though there weren't, I was corrected.

And anyway, I could have slipped on the ice. I could have been struck by a car. Would it have been worth the risk? Oh, it would have, it would have, if it meant otherwise losing my dear, sweet dog. But I couldn't budge, stuck there behind the

guardrail watching Charlie's tail flounc-
ing away. He disappeared down the em-
bankment on the other side of the freeway,
where there was a frozen marsh. I was much
too frightened to even scream or shut my
eyes or breathe. When I tried to whistle,
my mouth wouldn't work. It was like a
nightmare, when the hatchet man is coming for you and you want to scream, but
you can't. All I could do was wave to the
few cars driving by with my little red gloves,
like a fool, tears beading at the corners
of my eyes from both the cold wind and
my terror.

But then Charlie returned. He came
scuttling back at full speed across the ice,
catching a stretch of complete stillness on
the freeway, thank heavens. He carried the
dead bird—a meadowlark—softly between
his fangs and laid it at my feet and sat next
to it. "Good boy," I said, embarrassed by
my unruly emotions even in front of my
own dog. I dried my tears and embraced
him and held his neck in my arms and
kissed his head. His breath in the cold was
like a steam engine, his heart thumping.

Oh, how I loved him. How much life there was rumbling in that furry thing just astounded me.

Since then, I'd taught Charlie to fetch sticks and neon yellow tennis balls that turned brown and soggy with saliva, then gray and cracked, rolling under the front seat of the car, where I'd forget them. "This is a retriever, some bastard combination of Labrador and Weimaraner," the vet in Monlith had told me. That morning with the meadowlark was, perhaps, a significant day for Charlie. He discovered his innate purpose, some instinct kicked in. But what could I possibly want with that dead bird? I hadn't shot it down, nobody had. It was an odd thing to feel impelled to retrieve. Such are instincts. They aren't always reasonable, and often they lead us down dangerous paths.

I whistled, and Charlie came, a crumbling red shard of rotten wood poking out from his soft lips. I put the leash on him. "Just in case," I told him. He eyed me querulously, but didn't pull. I kept my eyes on the path on the walk home, one hand holding Charlie's leash, the other tucked inside my coat, grasping the note, to keep it safe, I told myself.

**It wasn't me.**

Who was this **me**? I wondered. It seemed unlikely that a woman would abandon a dead body in the woods, so I felt I could safely presume that the writer of the note, this **me,** this character, the **I** of the story, must be male. He seemed very sure of himself, indeed. **Nobody will ever know who killed her.** And how could he know that? And why would he bother to say it? Was it some kind of macho taunt? **I know something you don't know.** Men could be like that. But was murder an appropriate occasion to be so boastful? Magda was dead. That was no laughing matter. **Nobody will ever know who killed her.** What a silly way to ward off suspicion. How arrogant to think people are all so gullible. **I** wasn't. We were not **all** idiots. We weren't **all** lemmings, sheep, fools, like Walter always said all people were. If anybody knew who killed Magda, it was the "**I.**" Where was Magda now? Clearly **I** had been with her dead body while the note was being written. And so, what had become of her? Who had run off with her body? Had it been the killer? Had the killer come back for Magda after he, **I,** whatever, had written and laid down that note?

**My** note, I felt it was. And it was mine. I possessed it now, tried not to crinkle it in the warmth of my heavy down coat.

I'd need a name for this **me,** the writer of the note. At first I thought I'd need a name as just a placeholder, something lacking in personality so as not to describe the **me** too particularly, a name like the anonymous printed penmanship. It was important to keep an open mind. **I** could be anybody. But there was something to be gleaned from the serious and youthful ballpoint pen, the precise print, the strange nonadmission, the nobodyness of **I.** Blank. My husband's name, Walter, was one of my favorite names. Charlie was a good name for a dog, I thought. When we were feeling regal, I'd call him Charles. He did look regal sometimes, his ears perked up and eyes cast downward, like a king on his throne. But he was too good natured to be truly kingly. He wasn't a snobbish dog. He was no poodle or setter or spaniel. I'd wanted a manly breed, and when I'd gone into the kennel in Monlith, there he'd been. "Abandoned," they told me. "Discovered two months ago in a black duffel bag on the banks of the river. Barely three weeks old. The only one of the litter to survive." I spent a minute piecing that together. What horror! And then, what a miracle! From then on, I pictured myself as the one who had come upon the black duffel in the mud, under the bridge where the river thins, and that **I** had unzipped the bag to find a huddled swarm of heady, raisin-colored pups, only one of them breathing, and that one was mine. Charlie. Can you imagine abandoning such dear little creatures?

"Who would do something like that?"

"Times are tough," the woman told me.

I filled out the requisite forms, paid one hundred dollars for medical testing and vaccines, and signed a promise to get Charlie neutered, which I never did. I also didn't tell them that I'd be moving east, across seven states, all the way to Levant mere months later. These dog pounds, they need assurances. They want it in writing that a person will care for the animal and raise it in the right way. I promised not to abuse it or breed it, or let it run wild in the streets, as though a signature, a mere scribble on paper, could seal fate in place. I didn't want to neuter my dog. That seemed inhumane. But I signed my name on the contract, heart racing at this, one of very few deceptions I've ever enacted knowingly, blushing, trembling even at the thought that I'd be found out. "What kind of sick person doesn't neuter their mutt? What kind of perverse . . ." Naive, actually, to think that a mere signature was so binding. It's just a little ink on paper, just a scribble, my name. They couldn't come after me, drag me back to Monlith, simply because I'd moved a pen around.

So I got away all right. After Walter's funeral, I packed up the house in Monlith, bade farewell to the place and all it had put upon me. What a relief it was to get out of there, the house sold, and a new home in

Levant ready and waiting. In the pictures it was my dream home: a rustic cabin on a lake. The land needed work. There were some rotting trees, overgrowth, et cetera. I'd bought it sight unseen for a song. The place had been under foreclosure for six years. Times are tough, yes. And there I went. I tried not to think too much of the house back in Monlith, what the new owners were doing inside of it, how the porch had withstood the winter. And what my neighbors were saying. "She just took off, like a thief in the night." That wasn't true, though. I knew that. I was a good woman. I deserved some peace at last.

I thought some more about a name for this **me.** In the end, I settled on Blake. It was the kind of name parents were naming their boys those days. It had a twinge of pretension to it in that sense. Blake, as in the shaggy blond boy on the skateboard, the boy eating ice cream from the container, the boy with a squirt gun. Blake, clean your room. Blake, don't be late for dinner. Given these associations, the name was sneaky and a bit dumb, the kind of boy who would write, **It wasn't me.**

Strange, strange what the mind will do. My mind, Charlie's mind, sometimes I wondered just what the mind was, actually. It hardly made sense that it was something contained in my brain. How could I, simply by thinking that my feet were cold, be asking Charlie to shift his chin to cover them, which he did? Were we not of the same mind at such moments? And if there was a mind I shared with Charlie's, was there a separate mind I kept for myself? Whose mind was now at work, thinking of the note, imagining, debating, and remembering things as I walked down the path through the birch trees? Sometimes I felt that my mind was just a soft cloud of air around me, taking in whatever flew in, spinning it around, and then delivering it back out into the ether. Walter had always said I was sort of magical that way, a dreamer, his little dove. Walter and I had shared a mind, of course. Couples get that way. I think it has something to do with

sharing a bed. The mind, untethered during sleep, travels up and away, dancing,
sometimes in partners. Things pass back
and forth in dreams. When I dreamt of
Walter now, he was young again. He was
young still in my mind. I still expected
him, at times, to come through the door
with a bouquet of roses, carrying in the
sweet smell of his cigars, his hands on the
rustling cellophane so tender and strong.
"For you, my dove," he'd say. And if not
roses, then a book he thought I'd like. Or
a new record, or a perfect peach or pear. I
missed his thoughtful gifts, little surprises
pulled from the pocket of his overcoat.

I suppose my cabin in Levant was
Walter's final gift to me. I'd used the insur-
ance money to buy it, and to move. Profit
from the sale of the house in Monlith
would keep me fed until I died. And there
was also money in savings. Walter had
planned well for retirement. He was always
scrimping and saving, which made the
little gifts he gave me all the more lovely.
Roses were expensive, after all. "These cost
an arm and a leg," he said. "I hopped home

like a cripple." He'd have found my cabin cheap and small. He liked big, wide-open spaces. He loved it in Monlith, the plains, the metallic hills of rock, the cold river. I missed Walter. The big house became preposterous without him. When the cabin in Levant presented itself, it was a relief. I felt I needed to hide a little. My mind needed a smaller world to roam.

I thought of that dead meadowlark in Monlith again. It was yellow bellied, beautiful, like a jewel against the pale, frozen gravel. A gift. Strange, strange. Had Charlie thought it would cheer me up? I'd left it there where Charlie had dropped it, and took him by the collar and steered us back home, straining my shoulder, but there was no other way, the leash was ruined. After that, I read books on how to train him. Between packing up the house and signing more papers and so on, Charlie and I bonded and I taught him to obey me. He attuned himself to me and I to him. This was how our minds melded. The books confirmed that a dog should never sleep with its master. At first, we abided by this rule, but when we drove out east, staying in those roadside motels along the way, he crawled in and I couldn't stop him. I worried that the move would traumatize him. A little comfort did us both a lot of good. The open road is such a lonely place. In Levant, we did tend to sleep together, Charlie even nestling down under the covers with me when it was cold. But in the summer, he'd be at the foot of the bed, or off the bed entirely, splayed out in the cool shadows of the dining table downstairs. He was better on the leash now, though I rarely used it. I carried it with me when we went for walks, in case we came upon some wild animal, and Charlie was moved to attack it. I knew that he could be vicious if he wanted to, if someone was threatening me, if something bad happened. That was a comfort, too. Charlie, my bodyguard. If there was a madman on the prowl, Magda's killer, whoever, Charlie would attack. His head hit only about midthigh, but he was stately enough, broad shouldered, seventy-eight pounds of muscle and fine pale-brown fur. I'd seen him gnash his teeth and growl only once, at a rattlesnake back in Monlith. It took a lot to rile him up. I heard there were bears around Levant, but I didn't believe it. I'd seen dead foxes on the road. Also rabbits, raccoons, opossums. At dawn, apart from birds and small rodents, the only other souls out were the gentle whitetail deer. They hid behind trees, stock still as Charlie and I passed by. Out of respect, I tried not to look at them in the eye, and I'd trained Charlie to leave them alone, too. It must be nice to think you can become invisible just by standing still. They were beautiful deer, some as big as horses. What a nice life they must have, I thought. It was so quiet in the woods, sometimes I could hear them breathing.

Blake must have come through in the last twenty-four hours, I figured, since Charlie and I had been there the morning before, and there'd been nothing, no note. As we headed home, I saw no strange footprints, no white fringe or confetti from the ripped-off edge of Blake's spiral notebook. It had been a whole year now that I'd been in Levant, and those woods felt like they belonged to me and Charlie. Perhaps more than Magda's murder, it began to bother me that there had been someone else out there, in my woods, touching my rocks, walking down the path I'd been wearing and widening through the birch woods. An invasion. It was like coming home late, going to bed, and waking up to find that at some point in the night, someone had been in your kitchen, had been eating your food, reading your books, wiping his mouth with your cloth napkins, staring at his strange face in your bathroom mirror. I could imagine what fury and fear I'd feel discovering that he'd left the butter out on the counter, a crust of bread, to say nothing of a bloody knife in the sink, or a knife that had been used and washed and set in the rack to dry. **Nobody will ever know. . . .** It could drive a person crazy if something like that happened. You might never sleep again, might never again feel safe in your own home. Imagine all the questions you'd have, and only yourself to ask. The intruder could be in the house still. My God, he could be crouched

behind the kitchen door, and there you'd
be, standing in your socked feet and bath-
robe, agog at the knife glinting in the rack.
Had you used it to chop onions? Had you
forgotten that you'd wandered down for a
midnight snack, left the knife out, et cetera? Were you still dreaming? Was I?

No, no. This was real. Here was Charlie,
here was the ground, the air, the trees, the
sky above, the sweet green buds of leaves
quaking from the branches, pushing forward into life, come what may. I knew
these woods. I knew my cabin, the lake,
the pines, the road. I was the only person
to walk through the birch woods on a regular basis. The neighbors were far enough
to have their own birch woods, their own
paths. And why would anybody come all
the way up here, just to walk on my path?
Why would Blake have come, other than
for me? It was no mistake. The note was a
letter. Who else but me would have found
it? I had been chosen. It may just as well
have been addressed to me. **Dear Vesta.
I've been watching you. . . .**
Was Blake watching me even now as I

hurried out of the woods? I could imagine a teenage boy, just growing out of the doughy adolescent mask that hid his deviance. Did it give him some strange pleasure to see me so alarmed? Was his mind mingling with my mind somehow, planting these thoughts, these imaginings and reasonings? **Dear Vesta. I know where you live.** Suppose the woods had never been mine at all. Suppose **I'd** been the invader, and Blake, pushed to act finally, had sent me this message to scare me off, to ruin my world so that he could have it all to himself. My mind wrangled the possibilities. As we walked, I took the note out again to read it. **Her name was Magda.** That much still was true.

The sun was up now as we crossed the edge of the woods. The day ahead was bright and clear. There was no dark, brooding cloud, no sharp tang of storm in the fresh spring air. There was nothing to get tense about, nothing at my back, no need to run. So I found a note. So what? It couldn't hurt me. Magda, if she had been a threat, was dead and gone. And Blake claimed, at least, that he was no killer. There it was in black and white: **It wasn't me.** I could choose to believe it. There was nothing to fear. It was just a piece of paper, words on a page. Silly to get so invested. Stupid even. **Stupid.**

Down the hill we went, and across the road and up the gravel path to the cabin. At the door, I dropped the leash and wiped Charlie's feet with a rag, as I always did, holding the note between my lips, folding my lips inward so as not to wet the paper. Charlie looked up at me, annoyed but unperturbed. Certainly, if there was anything to fear, the hair on the back of Charlie's neck would be standing on edge, a sharp ridge to indicate danger, the threat of death. I rubbed his velvet ears. We went inside.

It was still cool and dark in the kitchen, which faced westward onto the gravel path and the little garden. I'd recently started tilling the soil in the clearing just outside the kitchen windows. I hoped to plant flowers, maybe tomatoes, squash, carrots. I'd never had a garden before. The earth in Monlith had been too dry. Nothing would have grown out there in that stale, red dirt. But in Levant, where it was green and pretty, I felt inspired to bring something new to life. I stood at the sink and looked out through the window, picturing how my garden would grow. Across from the raked-up dirt, there were spindly and rotted horsehair ropes hanging from a thick branch of the one large sycamore on the property. These were remnants of a swing, I supposed, installed back when the place had been a summer camp for Girl Scouts. The boathouse had been torn down, but my cabin, the main structure where the girls learned crafts and ate their meals, had endured. I had found rusted bobby pins, thimbles, jacks, broken knitting needles, small scissors fit for children's hands in the soil, wedged in between the grubs and earthworms. Those little artifacts must have been twenty or thirty years old by then, maybe older. Besides the sycamore and a few splintery stumps of rotted oaks, the trees on my property were all tall pines, mostly eastern whites. I had borrowed a book from the library and meant to study up on the local flora but it had been too scientific, too technical, not enough pictures to hold my attention. I had no sensitivity to science. Walter and his rational mind had exhausted my patience for that kind of mental busywork. Since his death, I'd grown to be more poetic in my thinking. Too much magic was dashed by cold logic.

If those birch woods across the road were good for dawn walks, my old pines were more for midnight. Shut in under their dark canopy of thick branches, sound was dampened by the nesty carpet of dried pine needles underfoot. The space the pines made was like an interior, like my den, a place where you'd sit and read or listen to records. A glass of bourbon, a warm wool sweater, a green glass desk lamp, a dark mantel, these things would have done nicely there. I didn't go very deep into the pines, however. Twice I'd wandered more than a quarter of a mile deep, and both times I became short of breath. There was something I was allergic to out there, some mold or spore, I guessed. Those thick groves of pines would keep me safe, I'd thought; the poisonous air would force any ne'er-do-well to retreat. But now that Magda had been murdered, I was not so sure.

Charlie came and rubbed his face against my knee, as though he sensed my anxiety. Sweet creature. Would I need a gun? An alarm system? Since I had moved in, I'd always left the door unlocked. I had nothing anyone would care to steal, anyway. But now, I felt the pine woods might actually invite danger. If there was a good place to hide, it was in the thick of those trees. That was where the killer was, I imagined, crouching in the shadows, biding his time until he struck again. My throat clenched. I dared myself to turn around, to look back over my shoulder through the kitchen window at the pines, but I could not. Someone could be standing there—I pictured Blake in oversized gym shorts and a blood-splattered T-shirt, a surly, skinny teen with a stunned, possessed look on his face. I held the note in my hands. **Her name was Magda.** Then I folded it defiantly and slipped it under a pile of mail on the table by the door. Leave it alone. Come on now, Vesta, I told myself. It will be there later, if you get bored. You've done enough imagining for one morning. Don't make trouble for yourself. Just go on about your day.

I turned on the overhead light, took off my boots, and hung up my coat, Charlie whining at my heels, hungry for breakfast. "I know, I know." Everything in the kitchen was as I'd left it. Coffee can upside down on the counter to remind myself to go buy more. Clean dishes in the rack, one plate, one cup, the usual mess of silverware, no butcher knife. The radio was on, as it always was when I left the house. That was a habit I'd picked up long ago. When we were newly married and still young and poor—Walter slaving over his dissertation, me working as a secretary in a medical billing office—we lived in a city apartment and played the radio to muffle the noises of our neighbors coming through the walls. Walter thought it wise to leave it on anytime we went out at night, to ward off burglars. I found it a comfort to come home to music playing, or a news report. **Welcome back,** the announcers said. And if I ever had to leave Charlie alone at home, I liked knowing that he wasn't just sitting in the dreary silence there, but keeping up with culture and current events, or listening to Bach or Verdi or Celtic music. **If you're just joining us . . .** But I rarely left Charlie alone in Levant. We were attached at the hip, as they say. **This just in . . .**

I heated a pot of chicken stew with rice on the stove and ladled it out into Charlie's food bowl on the kitchen floor. I had been feeding him leftovers since we'd moved to Levant. As a result, I only cooked things we both liked, especially in winter: stews, roasts, sweet potatoes, gravy. On this home-cooked diet, Charlie was calmer, his eyes brighter, his whole presence clearer. I knew he appreciated my cooking. You see, these were the simple things that gave me pleasure: I fed my dog. I looked out the den windows at the water, peaceful and pale under the morning sun. There was my little rowboat still tied to the dock. I had yet to take it out to the island in the middle of the lake that spring. The oars were right there in the den, leaning against the wall. Over the summer, I'd been so proud to row around and look back at the land, at all my property. It was mine. I owned it, this gorgeous pocket of planet Earth. It belonged only to me. And the island with its strange promontory and perilous rocks, a few lone pines, a blueberry bush, and a clearing just big enough to lay a blanket down, all of that belonged to me, too. I took great comfort in ownership. Nobody could ever interfere. The deed was in my name alone, all twelve acres. I hadn't even seen it all, because of my allergy to the pines.

The responsibility of maintaining the property had been daunting at first, but I'd managed all right. I still had to call someone to come remove that dock. It was sunken down on one side, useless. I'd managed to drag it out of the water by tying the metal steps to the rear bumper of my car with twine, but the thing had flipped and the soft old wood had cracked in places. I'd covered it with a tarp but the snow made it worse, all warped and splintered. I had no use for the dock anyway. Usually I waded into the water and got into the rowboat that way.

Charlie lapped at his bowl of water. I heated leftover coffee from the fridge in a pot on the stove. "We've had quite a morning, haven't we?" I said. "A little horror story. Gets the blood flowing, right?" Charlie, hearing my enthusiasm, trotted up to me, his nails scratching the wooden floor. I knelt down to him, and he reared up on his haunches and put his front paws on my shoulders. "Oh, you want to dance?" I held his paws in my hands, the pads soft and pink, and steered him to and fro around the kitchen. It wasn't his favorite thing, but he was a good sport. When I let go of his paws, he butted his head against my thighs, a kind of punctuation, and went back to his bowl of water. I got my coffee and a bagel from the fridge and went to sit in the breakfast nook, where I could look out at the water. I kept a pad of paper and a pen there to plan out each day.

The bagels I had every morning for breakfast were from the supermarket and came precut in a package of half a dozen. They weren't particularly healthy—bleached flour, full of preservatives—nor were they very tasty. They were chewy and dry, and sweet in a way bagels ought not be. But I liked them anyway. I hadn't bought myself a toaster. It seemed like an unnecessary luxury when I had a perfectly good oven. But who wants to heat an entire oven just to warm a bad bagel? It didn't matter. I ate them cold, one every morning, Tuesday through Sunday. Monday mornings, when I'd run out of bagels, I drove into Bethsmane and got a donut and coffee at the bakery and did my shopping for the week at the supermarket. I used the occasion to mosey around town, acting busy, though I had no real purpose. That was how life seemed to be—finding things to do to pass the time. The less I'd looked at the clock, the better I knew I'd enjoyed my day. Sometimes I stopped at the Bethsmane library, the post office, the hardware store. Other than those Monday morning escapades, I rarely went to town. Each day was like the day before, apart from the dwindling number of bagels, and the varying weather. I liked the storms that whisked in and out in the spring. The year before, I'd spent many rainy days indoors, mesmerized by the turbulence in the lake, the splatter of water flung on the roof and at the windows. Those days, my list of things to do was short: Read, Nap, Eat. The pad of paper I used to plan my days was legal size, the pages much longer than the paper Blake had used to write the note. But never mind that, I told myself. Each day I wrote out what I'd do, and each day I usually abandoned my plan halfway through.

**Walk.**
**Breakfast.**
**Garden.**
**Lunch.**
**Boat.**
**Hammock.**
**Wine.**

**Puzzle.**
**Bath.**
**Dinner.**
**Read.**
**Bed.**

I had no television to distract me. Watching television had always made me antsy. Walter said it put me in a mood. He was right. I could never focus and enjoy things because I always felt I had a better idea than what I saw on the screen, and I'd busy my mind with that, and become excited and have to get up and walk around. I felt I was wasting my life away sitting and staring at the lesser version onscreen. Reading was different, of course. I liked books. Books were quiet. They wouldn't scream in my face or get offended if I gave up on them. If I didn't like what I read, I could throw the book across the room. I could burn it in my fireplace. I could rip out the pages and use them to blow my nose, or in the bathroom. I never did any of that, of course—most of the books I read came from the library. When I didn't like something, I just shut the book and put it on the table by the door, spine facing the wall so that I wouldn't have to look at it again. There was great satisfaction in shoving a bad book through the return slot and hearing it splat against the other books in the bin on the other side of the librarian's desk. "You can just hand that to me," the librarian said. Oh no, I liked to shove it through. It made me feel powerful.

"Oh, forgive me, I didn't see you there," I'd whisper.

That old library in Bethsmane was a small brick building with all the newest books in spinning racks like you'd have found at a Woolworth's. There was a very nice reading room that looked out onto a clearing. Some congressman who had grown up in the town had donated a large sum, a plaque proclaimed. On one side of the reading room there was a large desk with a row of fancy computers. Usually there were young people using them. The big leather armchairs were often empty. The people in the area weren't too keen on reading. The way I chose books was usually by their covers and titles. If a book was named something that sounded too general, too wide open, I figured it was a book written in generalities, and so I'd find it boring, and I'd expect my mind would wander off too much. The worst books were those that offered banal instructions on how to improve oneself. I looked at them sometimes, just to laugh at the silliness. "Eat this and feel happy." That was the usual gist. Sometimes I looked for books I'd heard being reviewed on public radio. It was hard to separate the opinions of the reviewer from my own. And in that, it was easier to enjoy a book, feeling that I'd already made up my mind to like it. I didn't have to debate with myself so much, even if the book wasn't all that interesting.

As I ate my cold bagel and drank my coffee that morning at my table by the lakeside windows of my cabin, I wrote out my plan for the day. It was the same plan as for all the preceding days. Every day I rewrote it, after scratching out the identical plan I'd written the day before. Yesterdays were all failures. I didn't want to be taunted by the evidence. I forged ahead. There was work to be done in the garden. I had seeds ready to plant: carrots, turnips, dill, and cabbage on one side; sunflowers and forget-me-nots on the other. It wouldn't be the prettiest garden, but only I had to look at it. It was an experiment for me, and something to keep me grounded as the summer started. I'd owned that land for a year, and only now had I really started to get my hands into it. It made me feel happy and useful. There was plenty more digging to do, more weeds to pull, fertilizer to spread, and I could set the radio on the window ledge of the den and listen while I worked and while Charlie frolicked through the pines or splashed in the lake. With this plan set in my mind, I finished my coffee, put my dishes in the sink, and laced my boots back up. There, on the table by the door, was the mail, and the note from Blake I'd found in the birch woods. **Her name was Magda.** I opened the den window and turned the radio up. **Here is her dead body.**

"Charlie," I said, "let's get some air."

It wasn't as though I had forgotten the note. It had been there, writing itself over and over in my mind as I'd eaten breakfast and tried to think of other things. I'd managed to ward off any new thoughts about it in that time, but being close to it again, not even looking at it directly, just at the envelopes and papers I'd hidden it under, I could feel my heart swell and pound again. Oh, Magda. May you rest in peace, I said to her in my mind. What else can you do about a dead person than to wish them well? What more could have been expected of me in the situation? The note wasn't any kind of summons or proposition. It was a note of acknowledgment, not an invitation. Still, it left so much unexplained. **Nobody will ever know . . .** Such certainty. **Nobody will ever . . .** It was odd, his assurance. It occurred to me then, there might be more in the note than met the eye. Maybe I ought to be reading between the lines. **Her name was Magda. . . .**

Charlie licked my hand, interrupting my darkening reverie. Outside, the sun was shining. The garden called. No, I didn't have to read the note again. I could proceed with life. I would. I had to. I put my sun hat on, knotting the nylon strings under my throat. Anyway, who was I to ask questions? I was just a little old lady, peacefully waiting out the rest of my life, disturbing no one, and responsible for no one but myself and my dog.

"Let's go," I said.

Charlie bounded out past me as soon as I opened the door. I watched as he scampered across the gravel path and down the slight slope toward the lake. He pawed the wet dirt there and splashed a bit in the shallow waters. It was still too cold for me to go swimming, but Charlie was impervious to the cold. Even in the winter, when the thermostat on the kitchen window read in the single digits, he'd frolic out there in the snow until his paws and belly were raw and red, then come back huffing and puffing and curl up on the rug in front of the fireplace. He was so dear. He was so human sometimes, rolling his eyes and yawning like Walter would when I was uneasy after dinner, as though to say, "Come relax here with me on the couch, let my body soothe you, it's all right." I could hear Charlie prancing around while I worked in the garden. He disappeared out there for long jags, chasing squirrels through the thick of the pines, looping back to me once in a while for a kiss and a little pet, for my sake, it seemed. He didn't need me. Now that it was spring, he spent most of his time outdoors. I had to coax him in with treats and whistles when I wanted his company during the day. I never worried that he'd run away. By then I knew, he was mine. There were no greener pastures. He would always come when I called. He was like a teenager, confident and naive, exploring his world as though he owned it. His spirit was joyful and unworried. It seemed to me that he'd forgotten his early trauma with his siblings in the duffel bag, those poor sweet creatures. And how nice it was to know that one could forget such things. We are resilient. We suffer, heal, and proceed. Proceed, proceed, I told myself, taking up the trowel.

The dirt was cool and gritty, and though

I'd never learned much about planting and nursing, giving life to much of anything, I felt that my work in the garden was productive, sprinkling seeds and covering them, raking the unbroken ground, sifting through the clumps, and so forth.

Besides the weekly book reviewer on public radio, the radio in Levant was all Christian sermons, or pop music, or dark rock 'n' roll played on the station broadcast from the community college a few towns over. Late at night, if I couldn't sleep, I'd listen to the Christian call-in hotline. People would ask questions about Scripture, and occasionally for advice about how to handle some difficult situation in their lives in a good Christian way. It fascinated me that strangers would trust "Pastor Jimmy" with such serious matters, had no qualms about airing their dirty laundry over the radio waves. Some of them even gave their last names and the towns they lived in. "This is Patricia Fisher from New Ashford." "My name is Reynold Owens, and I live out here in Goshen Hills." "Yes, hello. This is

Lacey Gardner calling in from Amity. I think you know my husband?"

"Mrs. Gardner, hello. How is Kenneth? How is his health these days?"

Maybe one night I'd hear Blake call in. "You don't know me," he'd say. "But I have a problem. It's Magda. She's dead. Nobody will ever know . . ."

"Magda, what a strange name," Pastor Jimmy would say.

My name was also strange. All my life people had asked me, "What kind of name is Vesta Gul?"

"Vesta is an old family name. My mother's mother," I would tell them. "People call me Vi sometimes. My friends do. And Gul was my husband's name. It means 'rose' in Turkish. But he was from Germany."

"Is that your accent? It's a German accent?" asked the woman at the bank in Bethsmane. Walter did have a German accent, but I had none. I'd grown up in Horseneck. I was a normal person. I was like everybody else. If I had any accent, it was the accent of having no accent. Most people in Levant spoke with a rural drawl, sometimes so thick I could hardly parse out the strains of conversation I overheard now and then in town, or at the gas station where I filled up once a month. My Monday morning trips into town put me in touch with just a few shop clerks, the checkout girls at the grocery store, the gentle old man at the bakery. "Plain or glazed, today?" he'd ask.

"Plain, please," and "yes," and "thank you" were all I had to say. At the library, it was easy to be silent. Just a nod here, a smile there. Charlie was the one I talked to, and much of the time we were silent together, just sharing the mind space between us, feeling things back and forth.

**Her name was Magda.** Magda had an odd, rubbery ring to it, like **magma,** or **madman.** Thick and unguent and unruly. Or **magnum,** a word that for me conjured up a smoking gun, or a box of prophylactics, things I would never think about. **Her name was Magda.** Magda was just her nickname, I surmised. Blake must have known her well. Why else would he feel moved to attend to her dead body? He must have loved her. But he hadn't loved her enough to make a big stink over her death. The only stink Blake had made had been for me.

I took off my gardening gloves and tore open the packet of forget-me-not seeds. They were surprisingly big, the size of small ticks, shaped like raindrops but prickly, like burs. I pinched a few between my fingers and dropped them in a hole I'd poked into the dirt with my finger. It seemed unbelievable that these tiny things would someday bloom into little blue flowers, according to the package. The label said simply that they grow in average soil, need little attention, and take a week or two to germinate. How long would it take for the flowers to bloom? I wondered. Could I wait that long? I imagined the next two weeks, waiting anxiously for the little green stems to sprout out of the ground. It might drive me mad to sit there and stare. I'd manage somehow. I'd think of something to keep me busy. A wave of impatience came over me. It was new, this feeling. Somehow it had eluded me all winter. I'd fallen into a kind of dreamland while the world had frozen over and grown thin, days so short they vanished as soon as the coffee was made. My mind had become eerily gray and peaceful, as if I'd been hibernating from November through April. But the days were growing longer now. Dawn was earlier, dusk was later. There was more time to be up and alive. A tide of passion was rising. Before Walter had died, I'd taken pills to soothe my nerves. But when he'd died, I felt it was disrespectful to try to numb away my grief, so I'd flushed them down the toilet. In the garden, I momentarily regretted that. Lorazepam was the name. If I wanted any now, I'd have to go beg some Bethsmane clinician. You can imagine how he'd look at me. No, I couldn't bear to put up with that kind of humiliation. I would brave my nerves on my own.

I finished planting the seeds, covered all my buried treasures in a thin layer of topsoil and used the hose to spray a fine mist over the little garden plot. It wasn't the ideal place to grow a garden, I knew. Better outside the den windows, or off the narrow patio that faced north, toward the shed. Next summer I'd strategize. I'd be smarter by then, I thought. For now, I was pleased that I'd accomplished what I'd set out to do. I collected my tools into the red plastic pail and threw a rock I'd unearthed into the pine woods so I wouldn't trip on it. Charlie, seeing the gesture from afar, galloped up from the lake, wanting to play.

I threw him a stick. It soared through the air and skidded deep into the pines. Charlie went after it, deftly but at a respectable pace. He was calm and happy enough not to be hysterical. He knew it was just a stick, after all, and not a hunting rifle firing at some grouse or hare or marten. There was no bleeding body tumbling through the underbrush to snag and deliver. He took his time. In the moments that I was alone there, waiting for Charlie to come prancing back with the stick between his teeth, a gust of cold swept through as a cloud covered the sun, and I shivered and felt a little melancholy, and my mind drifted once more to Walter. It was a simple thought: He was gone and would never return. He was deceased. He was only ashes now, sitting in the bronze urn on my bedside table on the second floor, which was just a loft area over the kitchen, with a window above my headboard so I could gaze up at the stars over the lake at night. The loft wasn't meant to hold much weight, so all I had up there was the bed and table. Any more and I feared the floor would give way and we'd go crashing. When Charlie tossed and turned at night, I could hear the beams creaking. Not that I was truly worried. I slept so well in Levant. It was deadly quiet, just a few loons cooing. I had held onto Walter's ashes for longer than I thought I would. I'd brought them out to Levant with the idea that I could scatter them in the lake— my lake—and have him disintegrate into the water so that I would always have him there, lapping at my feet, enveloping me when I swam, or tickling my fingers as I grazed the surface on my boat rides to and from the little island—my island. But I hadn't scattered them yet. Soon, soon, I told myself. When it gets warmer.

I whistled for Charlie. I could hear him scrambling around, probably pawing through the dry, slippery pine needles. Charlie had never met Walter. He might have been born the day Walter had died, in fact. I'd never done the math before, but now it seemed to make sense—one life vanishes, another arrives. **Nobody will ever know who killed her.** I knew what had killed Walter. It wasn't something I liked to remember. Those last nights in the Monlith hospital ward, how the nurses looked down on me pityingly, the doctors idle in the doorway. "Any day now," they kept telling me, as though Walter's death was taking too long, and I'd been acting impatient for it. As though death were something to wait for at all. No, I wasn't that type of woman. I wouldn't wait for death. I would hold on tight to life, caress Walter's

hand, pet his head, kiss him on the cheek
and forehead, as long as there was life still
in him. I had no idea if he could hear me
when I spoke. I talked a lot while he was
dying. I thought that was what I was supposed to do. We'd spent nearly four whole
decades together in Monlith, barely talking some days, not out of spite, but just
that there seemed to be no need. We were
of a mind. We knew each other. But then,
suddenly, when Walter was dying, I had so
much to say. I cried and wished and prayed,
though I'd never been a praying woman
before. "Oh, please, God, give him one
more day," I said, head down next to his on
the starched, white pillow, a sour chemical
smell emanating from his wan body. And
each day, my prayers were answered. Until
the day they weren't. And then he was in
a better place, as they say. But not quite
gone. His body was there, lying in repose
quite calmly, as though he'd had a hard
day at work and had taken, as sometimes
he'd been wont to do, a sleeping pill or one
of my lorazepams. "Is he just sleeping?"

I asked the nurse. How silly. "I was just talking to him like I always do, and then that machine started . . ." I'd done my best. I'd been as interesting as I could. I'd tried very hard to keep Walter there in the room with me. Years before his illness, I'd said, "If you die before me, please, send me a sign. However you can. Just let me know that you're around, and that it's all right over there, wherever we go when we die." He must have thought I was just joking. "Yes, yes, Vesta. I will. Don't worry." I tried to remind him in the hospital room. I even spoke up to the air in the room, as though Walter had left his body and was in the space above his bed, floating in the cold, sterile air of the hospital. Over the next few minutes, his body went slack in a way I'd never seen it. His hands became cold. A blur.

Charlie came back, scampering now not with the stick I'd thrown out there, but a rotting red branch of fallen pine, feathery almost in its soft state of degradation. "Good boy," I called him, and patted my pocket for a treat. They were in my coat, however, which I'd hung up after the dawn walk. The treats were crumbled now, most likely, between the black rocks that had held the note down on the ground. **Her name was Magda.** I shook the thought away. All I had to do now was go back inside, rest for a while, and begin preparing lunch for myself out of the last bits of food I had to tide me over until the next day, which was Monday, when I'd go to town for my weekly shopping. I took the radio out of the window and turned it off. Charlie was standing in the open doorway with his big rotting tree branch, not wanting to drop it and come in.

"My name was Magda." I imagined a voice on the Christian call-in show. "Nobody knows who killed me. It wasn't Blake."

"Good morning, Magda," Pastor Jimmy might say. "I'm sorry to hear about your problem. I hear a deep sadness in your voice today. If it is any consolation, you are not alone. All of God's creatures die. Death is a natural part of the life cycle, and it is not an end. Don't for a minute see it as something to feel bad about. May I ask, where are you calling from? And how might I help you? Do you have a question to ask?"

"There's my dead body, out there in the birch woods, across from the old Girl Scout camp that now belongs to Vesta Gul. I don't know if there's anything you can do for me, pastor. I just thought I'd call in."

"Vesta Gul, you say? What kind of name is that?"

No answer.

"Do you have a message for Mrs. Gul, in case she's listening?"

"Please, come and find me. I'm out here, somewhere near you. You're the only one who knows."

What silliness.

The voice I'd imagined was more like my voice—polite, a singsong lightness under the gravity of death. Magda would be more high strung. Any dead girl ought to sound hysterical. I had never allowed myself to sound that way. Walter nipped my moods in the bud the moment a twinge of anything untoward showed on my face.

I shook my head and opened the refrigerator.

"Charlie," I said, "let's go to town. All this food is old and yucky. And I want a good cup of coffee. My head is spinning."

And with that, I wiped off Charlie's paws and grabbed my coat and purse and Charlie's leash from the hook on the wall, and we tucked into the car. I didn't lock the cabin door. No, I wouldn't. There was nobody lurking out there in the woods, I told myself. Suspicion invites danger, doesn't it? Keep the imagination soft and happy, and only good things will come. If there was somebody lurking out there in the woods, it was only Magda. And she was dead. **Here is her dead body.** Was that so terrible? There were dead things everywhere—leaves, grass, bugs, all of God's creatures died, and the ones in the woods—the squirrels, the mice, even the deer and bunny rabbits—none of **them** were ever found. None of **them** were ever buried. What's so wrong about that? Nothing. God's green Earth, I told myself.

We drove out down the gravel path and

onto the dirt road and onto Route 17. I didn't even look up at the birch woods as we passed them. I didn't want to. I didn't need to. And there was nothing I needed to do that I didn't want to do. That was why I came here, to Levant—only to do exactly what I wanted.

# Two

The town of Bethsmane was ten miles from my cabin. I rolled down my window and then Charlie's, and I stuck out my elbow and he stuck out his snout, eyes shut in what looked like ecstasy at the thrill of the wind rushing through. I swung around the lake, passing my one neighbor's overgrown driveway marked with a rusted mailbox at a sharp curve in the road. The dark pine woods spread up to Route 17, which I took going east, past the small store with its single gas pump and signs for hot coffee, milk, eggs, live bait, and ice. I had only been there a handful of times to buy matches and basic provisions during the winter, when I'd been too sleepy and worried about driving over the icy roads as far as Bethsmane. The man who worked there was middle aged and quiet and badly scarred. The left side of his face was deeply pocked, and down the middle of his face, over his nose, which was just a little jump with two downward-facing holes, was a rectangle of skin laid over his face like a carpet. If you'd asked me to guess where it had come from, I would have said it was from the man's forearm, since it seemed to have been shaved down and sunburnt and wrinkled in a way that men's arms would get, if they were to shave them. That strange piece of skin was seamed up around the forehead and down both cheeks, like a ventriloquist's doll, and ended at his mouth, which was normal, maybe a bit browner than most. His chin seemed intact, unre-markable. When he turned to the left and only his right side was visible, he looked almost handsome, despite the lump of nose that in profile looked like a cat's. From the right, he had thick hair, his forehead and eye socket and cheekbones were finely

contoured, masculine, with one nice eye,
thoughtful and not unintelligent. His hair
was carefully combed, I noticed, perhaps
so much so because his hairline on the left
seemed to have been reconstructed. There
was a weird geometry to it with strands
not all flowing in the right direction. I
couldn't look at his left ear, like a candle
melted down to the bottom. And the nose.
It was really awful. It was hard to look him
in the eye as I'd paid. "Hunting accident,"
he'd said. I'd wondered since then how a
person gets shot in the head like that by
accident. I didn't know much, nothing
really, about guns and hunting. Rifles.
Buckshot. I'd heard those words. I knew
people hunted deer in the surrounding areas,
but it was forbidden in Levant. Nobody
was hunting deer or anything else in the
birches, or in my pine woods. Signs were
posted. As I drove, I wondered whether it
was possible Magda had been killed by accident. Not every death was a murder, after
all. But was anything really done by accident? Pastor Jimmy, in attempting to soothe
a caller's anxiety, often proclaimed with

utter assurance that "nothing happens in God's universe by accident. Everything happens for a reason." That old line.

Bethsmane was ugly. There were "For Sale" signs on every other truck and mobile home. It seemed preposterous that someone would choose to live in such a place, inhabit one of the cheap aluminum-sided factory houses, send their children to school in the mornings, drive to work—Where? To do what?—then come home at night to sit on their couches and watch television. That was a sad thought. I pictured family dinners: green bean casserole, macaroni and cheese, glasses of orange soda and cheap beer, chocolate ice cream. That was not how I wanted to live.

I parked in the lot in front of Save-Rite and cracked the windows of the car for Charlie. "I'll be right back. Now don't you howl." Inside, I went quickly to the produce section. There was not a wide variety to choose from, and I always bought the same few things: one onion, two beefsteak tomatoes, which were cold and mealy, one greasy cucumber, one head of green cabbage, one head of iceberg lettuce, two carrots, two lemons, an apple, an orange, a bag of red grapes. From the chilly back end of the meat department I chose one whole chicken and a package of beef bones for Charlie. Then a carton of milk and a small container of cottage cheese. Then coffee and the half dozen bagels from a shelf by the bakery, where brightly decorated birthday cakes sat beside a fogged-up glass case of donuts. I watched a fat woman pull a small square of parchment from the dispenser, open the opaque lid of the glass case, and select what must have been a dozen chocolate-covered donuts, dropping each in the paper bag, licking her fingers and wiping them on her black wool coat, which was buttoned tight around her bulging midsection, the back flap gaping and splitting up the seam. This was one type of person I had come to recognize on my trips to Bethsmane: heavy women, big as cows, whose thick ankles seemed about to snap as they tottered up and down the aisles with their huge shopping carts filled with junk food. It was a Sunday afternoon. I wondered if that woman would be eating those donuts alone in front of her satellite television, projecting herself into the drama of her daytime soap operas, or idly wishing that she might win a new dinette set or a trip to Boca on **The Price Is Right.** I'd watched that show once at my dentist's office back in Monlith.

Had Magda been one of those fat women? I didn't get that impression. **Here is her dead body.** I pictured her teenaged, lithe and slouchy, with long black hair, an oversize letterman jacket with white leather sleeves, some patch on the back attesting ironically to her allegiance to a local sports team. Her legs would be long, too long for her jeans. A bit of skin would be visible in the gap from the cuffs of her jeans to her white socks. Her sneakers were black or blue and nondescript. Dirty and worn down, charmingly, I thought. She wasn't the kind of girl to walk around in high heels, pretend like she's some prize to be won. And yet she must have been special. A coolness, perhaps, and a rough, innate glamour. With a name like Magda, there must have been something exotic about her. I could relate to her in this way, as my parents had come over during the war, carrying with them their paranoia and strange persuasions. I could imagine that Magda's parents were immigrants, too, or perhaps simply loyal to their heritage in a way that most people here were not. "We'll call her Magda." Truly American parents wouldn't name their daughter that. I imagined that, like my parents, they were Eastern European, and cold, from a cold place with hard winters and old ladies in fur hats and shawls, cathedrals, thin soups, strong homemade liquor, a gray city world, or harsh farms and steep hills, a stray wolf that terrorized the town, et cetera. Perhaps Levant reminded Magda of home. She didn't mind the fat ladies at the supermarket, the cheap aluminum houses. She found the place beautiful, yes, but shadowed with a sad reminiscence of her past, her homeland. Levant was like a hiding place, a resting spot. It's very stressful to be plucked from one world and plunked down in another. One loses her roots, no matter how hard traditions are clung to. I'd seen it in my parents—traditions change. Food, holidays, modes of dress. One assimilates, or forever lives as though in exile. Poor Magda, the adjustment must have been hard. And so, I felt I knew her. I was a stranger in Levant, too.

Walter was from Bremen. When he was tired or sick, the accent got thicker, **v**'s for **w**'s, **zo** and **ziss,** hissy and short when he got drunk, "Please, Vesta, go to bett." Perhaps Magda's mother tongue made an appearance as she pleaded for her life in the birch woods. "**Vie, vie?**" Where had she come from? Budapest, or Bucharest, or Belarus? Istanbul was too far east. Warsaw, or Prague. Belgrade?

My own parents had come from Valtura, a small town on the Adriatic. Farmers who sold their land before the war began in earnest, they came by boat with no plan at all. They had me late in life, raised me on the flatlands of Horseneck, where the only other immigrants were a family from China. Not that I minded much. I blended in fine at school. When everybody's poor, the little differences don't matter as much. People were homey in Horseneck and in Shinscreek, where we moved when I was in high school. I had a happy childhood. My parents never let me forget how lucky I was. They'd had a son before me who'd drowned in Valtura. "You were spared the peasant life" was how Walter explained it to me when he first met my parents. When we were engaged, we went to visit them in their little apartment in Shinscreek. It's not a very wonderful memory. I saw clearly how I had to abandon my roots in order to live a more comfortable life with Walter. It was an easy choice, but also a sad one. We both agreed we needn't complicate things by having children. Neither of us wanted any children.

Magda could have been my daughter, I thought briefly. Her age would make sense if I'd had her very late, too late, a fluke, an accident, a miracle baby. And that would have been the only kind of baby I'd ever have. Walter had forbidden me from using contraceptive pills. He said they sapped a woman's integrity. We had our methods. I left it up to Walter. It was messy but better than any alternatives I could think of.

I could imagine this daughter of mine as an adolescent, turning her back to me in defiance, running up the stairs in the old Monlith house. I could imagine her room, pretty wallpaper torn off on one side, notes and photo-booth strips and postcards pinned to the wall and stuck in the frame of her mirror over a bureau littered with gum wrappers and old cassette tapes, dog-eared vampire mysteries and detective novels, a rusted Swiss Army knife, a big dusty pinecone, a tube of cheap orange lipstick. "Leave me alone," I could imagine her mumbling if I knocked on her door while she was reading. I could imagine her calling me Mom, a long and irritated **ah**-sound. If only Charlie could learn to talk. I'd always wanted to be called something other than what my name is. Vesta, Miss Lesh, Mrs. Gul.

Magda's face in my mind seemed to me still hidden behind the curtain of silky black hair and smushed into the soft ground of the quiet birch woods. There were probably worms and maggots crawling up her lips and into her mouth. How could she talk at all with a mouth full of stuff like that? What might she even want to tell me? Her body would speak for itself, I guessed. She might have dark red polish on her fingernails. She might be wearing fake diamond earrings, a gift she'd received for her birthday. From some admirer, most likely. An older man. Not Blake, who was just a kid, and wouldn't have been the one to buy her diamonds. Her hair, splayed across the forest floor, would be damp by now, full of dead leaves and detritus, but I imagined it would still look glossy, vibrant. Such a young girl, maybe nineteen? Nineteen and a half at most. "Magda." I clucked to myself. A pity you had to die. What a dumb, cruel world. And yet it didn't seem to be a real world.

Not my world. Magda's world was dumb and cruel. Mine had a mysterious note in it, but otherwise was placid and mellow. Walter had told me stories of the war, and they were worse than vampire books. They didn't seem at all real either. It was dumb and cruel that anyone had to die at any moment they weren't ready for, if they still felt there was more life to live. Walter had been ready to die, I thought. He nearly did it on purpose. "I'm bored now, let's get this over with." That was his attitude.

You could imagine the deaths of these dull heifers roaming the Save-Rite, these sad mothers with nothing to do but eat and fold laundry with tiny, stubby fingers sticking out of their huge bloated hands. Their lives must feel like such ineffectual blither blather. Did they even think things to themselves? Why did they look so idiotic, like domesticated animals, chewing their cud until the slaughter, half asleep? I had to feel sorry for those women, imagining each of them strangled and bludgeoned deep in my birch woods, left to rot or to be eaten by wolves. A woman should be laid to rest with dignity, of course. No matter where she lives or what she does with herself. When I die, I thought suddenly, wistfully, bury me under an apple tree. I was carried away by the thought. And then it seemed ridiculous, which it was, as no one was listening. I chuckled to myself, raked my fingers through my white hair.

Magda couldn't be too pretty, I reasoned. Anyone too pretty would have had people out looking for her. She'd have admirers, sure. Every teenage girl had those. I would have worried about her going out at night, smoking in a tree house, or huffing paint—I'd read about that in a magazine, in line at the grocery store the week before. But she couldn't have been too popular or too beloved. She may not have been missed at all. Perhaps the people of Levant were even happy to overlook her absence. There might have been something about Magda that those folks didn't want to see. She may have been a nuisance, a burdensome personality that got under one's skin, but one would have a hard time describing exactly why. Nobody would ever question her absence, as though saying her name could invite her back, and everyone was happy that she was gone. Her parents in Belarus had been glad she'd left in the first place, fed up with her misery and complaints. They kicked her out, I imagined. "All you do is brush your hair and smoke cigarettes out the window," her mother may have said, stirring a pot of soup. "Go get a job. If you hate school so much, go out and do something." "You are ungrateful. You think your life is so hard because you aren't some whore on the television? Ugly girls find honest husbands. Thank God you aren't a beauty." Or her father, drunk off plum brandy or whatnot, sitting on a tap-estried sofa in front of his grainy television screen, a lace doily covering an old coffee table, said, "Get out of my house, Magda. I can't bear to look at you. You make me sick. Go to America if you're so miserable here with us. Go work in McDonald's." Maybe I was the only person who cared that Magda was gone. Blake had cared enough to leave a note, but was that really caring? If my friend was dead in the birch woods, I'd certainly have done more than leave a note. And so I would. I decided then and there: I would do more. I'm coming for you, Magda, I said in my mind. Nobody seemed to notice that my mindspace was so hectic as I paced the aisles of canned soups and boxed cereals. Nobody in the market seemed to notice me at all.

I got in line at the checkout and looked around at the townspeople. If any of them knew Magda, if they cared about her, they hadn't noticed she'd been gone. She hadn't shown up for work. Maybe she'd gone out, with Blake, I supposed, and they had gotten in some trouble. Blake again. What nerve he had, leaving Magda's body all alone. He must have been involved somehow. I wasn't an expert in crime, but I knew this much: Blake was a suspect. He had contact with Magda's dead body. He knew something. **It wasn't me.** His denial only made him seem scared and paranoid. And if I knew anything about paranoia, it was that it sprang from guilt and regret. Always. I'd seen it clear as day in Walter when we were having our troubles. "You're crazy," guilty people say. They try to dismiss your inquiries. "You're paranoic," Walter insisted. Guilty people will try to divert your attentions. "Vee vere just talkink! I vas just helping her!" he said. **Nobody will ever find her.** Blake was guilty of something, whether of murder or neglect or stupidity, I didn't know yet. If there were any actions to be taken, the first would be to find that boy. I had little to go on. But then again, the town was small. He was literate, that Blake. I knew that at least. And he had enough common sense to know if someone was alive or not. He must have felt Magda's wrist or throat. I wondered how long he'd waited, wishing or not wishing for her heart to beat. Three minutes without a pulse and you're dead. I knew that. But there'd been stories on the radio, I remembered, of people who had come back to life after hours, days even. "Jesus was dead and buried and three days later, he rose," Pastor Jimmy said. And what did it really mean to be dead, after all? If one is still alive for the first few minutes without a pulse, then a heartbeat is not necessarily the signpost for being alive. The heart isn't the gauge. Even when the heart dies, other organs continue to live. Then where is the line between alive and dead? It's the brain that dies when the heart stops pumping. Yes, this was true. The brain needs oxygen, which the heart and lungs deliver. And without the brain, there is no mind, doctors said: If the brain is dead, the person is gone. The mind is over. But what if the doctors were wrong? What if the mindspace was not something made by the brain, and what if it continued even after death? Oh, I could get carried away imagining all sorts of theories. At times I wondered, Walter, are you hearing all this? Was he still up there, sharing the mindspace with me? What would he think if he could see me in this new life in Levant, a single old lady in the woods, with a dog? Walter always hated dogs. How did I love a man who hated dogs? We all have our quirks and issues, I told myself.

So while Magda's heart may have stopped,

her skin and nails, her teeth even, they might still be living. I looked at my watch. It was nearly eleven already. Skin cells live how long, twelve hours? Had Magda been murdered yesterday, or after midnight? Or days ago? Only her dead body would tell. And who knows where her body got dragged to, off the path where it had once been. Maybe an animal had taken it. Could a bear abscond with an entire human being, leaving no trace of blood, no nothing? I could go back to the birch woods and look around some more, for evidence of the body, but I was frightened. Death was fine to think about, but to get too close I felt would infect me somehow. It would change me. Walter's dead body had been bad enough, and I hadn't seen him looking dead for very long. One moment his body was there, he was alive inside of it, and the next moment he wasn't. It was horrifying, just that. If I'd found Magda mangled and bloodied, I would have had a nervous attack. It might spoil my mind, I thought. I could go crazy. And I couldn't afford to do that. I had to take care of Charlie. My garden was already growing. And who was I? I was just one person, a woman of seventy-two. Could it be? Was I so old? I had problems of my own. I had my own plans, my own path to follow. I had to row out to the island. I had to fix something for supper. I had to read a book, to sweep, to brush Charlie's coat and look for ticks. Magda and Blake were not my problems.

Still, I had the note. It was the note that was the problem. It was evidence now, and I had it. If anything happened, if the police got involved, I would have to come forward. I'd have to confess, "Yes, I had it the whole time." And I'd lie, "Under here, beneath all these papers. Oh, I'm an old lady. I am forgetful. I barely even read it, thought it was just a piece of trash." Who would believe me? They'd put me in jail. Hiding evidence of a crime was a crime in itself, was it not? That note made me an accomplice, a suspect even. "Strange woman, an out-of-towner with a funny name." "What brings you to Levant?" The police had asked me that when I first moved into the cabin. Of the locals, they proved to be the least charming of all. Standing there in the doorway with their hands on their hips, as if I were some kind of threat to them. They had come to my cabin to intimidate me, I thought, and thus to indoctrinate me, so to speak, into the culture of Levant.

"Winters get cold out here. County does its best to clear the roads but a gal like you has to take precautions. Now if anything happens, you call us right away, okay?" They called me "Miss Gool."

"Gul," I said. "Like the ocean bird." And then, as though I thought this would soften them, I said, "But please just call me Vesta."

"You've got your landline working, ma'am?"

I said I'd get it up any day, though a year later, I still hadn't. I had no need for a phone. I had nobody to call, and nobody would ever call me. But those policemen were persistent. "Now, you aren't shacking up with any strange types, are you, no tenants? There's a special ordinance for tenants. You can't be renting this place out like a hotel, you know that, don't you? The county has strict rules." I shook my head. The only people who ever came to the cabin were my handymen. "And no little boyfriends?" I giggled, though I wished I hadn't. "And nobody's approached you? You see anything suspicious, if anyone tries to contact you, just know, people around here, sometimes they're up to no good. We've been having problems, youths, mostly, they get drunk and do stupid things. And then of course you've got the homemade narcotics. Nothing you need to concern yourself with. Just be aware. You know, it's a pretty spot you have here, but this isn't exactly a retirement community," they said.

I knew what they were saying. "Times are tough," I said and nodded. I held Charlie by the collar and stood and listened to the policemen say their piece.

"If you see anything strange, if anybody asks you any favors—"

"What kind of favors? Am I not allowed to be neighborly?"

"There's no cause for alarm," they said.

"Just be advised. There's good reason this land went for so cheap."

"Thank you," I said when they were done, and shut the door on them.

I never heard of any criminal activity. I'd been in Levant a whole year, and the worst thing I'd seen happen was a single car crash. A driver hit a tree on Route 17. I'd driven past the tow truck hitching up the wreck. But that was all. I hadn't liked those policemen, their flabby, parched faces, eyeing my home, my private space, with guns in their belts, badges gleaming, strutting around the acreage like they owned the place. Jealous, they were, that I'd had the cash to buy the camp. That was prime land, and I'd paid pennies on the dollar for it. If nobody in Levant or Bethsmane could afford it, they ought to be happy I'd saved it from ruin. Anyway, I paid my taxes. Those cops worked for me, after all. No, I wouldn't tell them about the note. If Magda's body got dredged up out of the lake, I'd burn the note and bury the ashes. I'd act shocked and horrified if they interviewed me for the local paper. "I can't believe it," I'd tell the reporter. "To think something like that could happen here, on my lake. . . . No, I saw nothing, heard nothing. I would have gone straight to the police if I had."

With my groceries in the backseat, I drove to the library. I returned my book about trees and a thick novel about pioneer women that had struck me as melodramatic. One of the public computers in the reading room was occupied by a couple whom I guessed were in their early twenties, though the people of the area tended to look about ten years past their actual ages. Even their children looked prematurely aged, so worn and bloated. No wonder, I thought, considering the kind of women who were feeding them. There was no outdoor recreation for kids that I'd seen, no playground, no jungle gym at the school. Monlith had had a public park by the school, and wherever you went there was something to occupy the children—crayons at the restaurants, coin-operated bucking broncos, even a petting zoo. If we'd had a child, it would have grown up well in Monlith. But it had never been a possibility. Pointless to even think about it. I stood and watched the two young people huddled in front of the flashing computer. Then I walked over, pulled out a free chair in front of a dimly lit screen, and cleared my throat. I looked around for the "on" button, but couldn't find it.

"Excuse me," I said. "Do you know how to turn this on?"

The girl—braces, eyes edged with deep crow's-feet, a mouth both lipless and fleshy somehow—darted a bony arm across my lap and flicked the dun-colored mouse on the soiled, gelatinous mousepad. The screen of my computer came to life, showing astral patterns, swirling like the northern lights I'd read about in **National Geographic.** A few icons on the screen blinked on.

"Thank you, dear," I told her.

"Uh-huh," she replied.

I looked for the internet, and managed

to use the mouse to click open the browser window, and typed in www.askjeeves.com, as I'd learned to do in a computer course Walter had encouraged me to sign up for, back when he was still alive enough to have good ideas, but already sick. "You need to embrace the future," he'd said. "Get to know what's out there. When I'm gone, there will be no need to keep living the way we have, with these old things. You'll move on. But you have to put some effort in, Vesta. You can't be lazy." He'd become caring and concerned for me once the diagnosis was certain. He may have feigned concern before then trying to divert my attention away from what he thought I might know about how he spent his time outside of the house. He was almost never home. I liked it when he got sick for that very reason. For years he'd ignored me. Then suddenly, I was the person he clung to.

The computer class had been taught by a man in his thirties, a child to me, and he'd spoken to me so gently, with such reassurance, guiding with his finger across the glowing screen to show me where to click, where to drag, how to delete, to select, to navigate. And so in the Levant library, I took kindly to the internet, and set off to have all my questions answered.

The first thing I wanted to know was whether Magda was a real person, if she'd even existed at all. I half expected to find a little obituary written up about her in the local paper. "Is Magda dead?" I Asked Jeeves. What I found were 626,000 web pages, the first dozen devoted to a tragic story of how a young British fan of what seemed to be a highly successful all-boy band, a girl who had devoted her life to "blogging" about the musical group, dropped dead one morning waiting for the school bus. She was only sixteen. "Magdalena Szablinksa collapsed, and then passed away." Well, that didn't help me.

Three more "Magda" web pages caught my eye. The first was Magda Gabor. She'd been Zsa Zsa's sister and dead for over twenty years already. For the last three decades of her life she'd been incapacitated by a stroke, poor woman. Six husbands. Hungarian, an actress and a socialite, whatever that meant. And that sister of hers. Of course this was not the Magda I was looking for.

The next Magda was an Italian opera singer who seemed to have done quite well for herself. Her last performances were in a single-woman opera, which to me meant she must have known something about a woman's power, a woman's need to have her voice heard, and so forth. What courage she had. This was a true pioneer, and not some skinny lady in an apron, milking a cow like in that dreary novel I'd just returned. This singing Magda lived to 104, and had only just died that last September. Poor Magda Olivero. She seemed far more worthy of the name than the others.

The last dead Magda I found was Magda Goebbels. I didn't need to read about her. If anything would give me nightmares, it was the story of this Magda. I clicked the window closed.

There was no use in consulting the Levant phone directory. I didn't know Magda's last name. So I Asked Jeeves, "Does anyone named Magda live in Levant?" and found an African American woman named Magda Levant, living in Lubbock, Texas. Then I tried "How about a Magdalena in Levant" and was directed to a listing for a house for sale in Chula Vista, California. That wasn't right. The couple on the computer next to me gathered their pens and paper—a composition notebook, no spiral wire between them—and left their computer screen on and flickering. When I glanced at it, it showed the web page of a local abortion clinic. Magda Goebbels indeed, I thought. The woman had poisoned her six children, and for what? To spare them the suffering of watching her being put on trial? I thought of Nuremberg, and how Walter's throat would fill with phlegm whenever something pertaining to the war and Hitler and the Nazis was on the radio. He'd cough and choke. "Turn the damn thing off!"

A twinge of sadness. If Walter were here, he'd know just what to do about the note.

He'd have a theory, fixed and finite, without any wavering clauses, no doubt, no panic. I loved how sure Walter was about things. I missed that. We didn't always agree, but it seemed that confidence and conviction could turn even a wrong answer into a right one. "Use logic, Vesta," he'd say when I expressed some flowery opinion. "It's either this or that. Decide and move forward. You spend so much time playing in your mind, like a sandbox. Everything just slipping through your fingers, nothing solid to hold."

I clicked my internet window closed. There were the northern lights again. Everything seemed spectral and foreboding. The reading room was empty and darkening now as clouds gathered outside the large picture windows. I felt very abandoned and lonely. It was momentary sadness, that was all, but just for that second, with Goebbels, and the tiny embryo in the belly of that girl, I was paralyzed with dread. Rare that I ever felt so bad. I felt I weighed several hundred pounds, like that waddling donut eater in Save-Rite. I could barely breathe, but I did turn back around to face my computer. The purple-cushioned swivel chair squeaked and groaned. The librarian had disappeared into some back room behind her desk. I was glad. I didn't want to be seen in such a state.

But I suppose from the outside I looked perfectly normal. Well, normal for me. I was still rather exotic looking here in Levant. They were all so ruddy and pale, Irish, I guessed. I looked like an old Gypsy in comparison. Nobody had a face like mine. In the black, starry sky of the computer screen, I regarded myself. I was still me, I was still Vesta, with all her beauty and funniness. Walter used to play a game when we sat across from each other at dinner. He'd take whatever book he'd lain aside on the table and use it to cover up the bottom half of my face, just covering the tip of my nose. "Breathtaking!" he'd say. And he was right. My eyes, my hair—soft and black back then—the contours of my cheekbones and eye sockets, my high nose, my surprising blue eyes, I was gorgeous. People would stop me in the street when I was young, in the city. I used to dress in such a way, people wanted to take my picture. These days, judging from the ads in the supermarket magazines, one has to be seven feet tall and have the face of a two-year-old to get anyone's attention. And time has wrinkled my skin enough so that the sharp edges of my skull—which used to be so fascinating—have softened, like a blanket thrown over a carved mahogany chair. After admiring my eyes, Walter would raise his book to cover the top half of my face so that only the bottom half showed. It was like a completely different face then: only the tip of my nose, which is a bit hooked, and my cheeks cinched down with frown lines—they were there even when I was young—and my tiny mouth, "so tiny, I must feed you like a sparrow," Walter said, picking a little pea off his plate—my jaw, long and exaggerated, like "the blade of a hockey stick."

I had a slight underbite, the dentist told me. "Who is this witch and where has she buried my wife?" Walter would say, gently stroking my throat. But it wasn't that the top of my face was good and bottom half was bad. It was just that they seemed so misaligned. The miracle was that when Walter took the book away, my face—both halves—would settle in so well together. "Perfection." There were children's books I'd seen that played the same game. You'd have a laugh trying to match up this bearded pirate's torso with that princess's shoulders with a lion's head, and so forth. I pictured my head on a man's body, my legs like the finned tail of a fish. Imagining this mishmash, I suddenly felt very uneasy. My face on the screen wobbled for a moment, and then the moving image went from northern lights to a flashing bright blue with a twisted white line of words swirling around it. I knew the name for this: "screensaver."

I should go, I thought. Charlie was waiting for me in the car, curled up, I imagined, on the backseat, the heat of his breath fogging up the windows. All I had to do was stand, cross the carpet into the foyer of the library, where the desk was, and exit through the old red door, watch my footing down the uneven brick path to the car in the parking lot. But it felt impossible. I felt glued down, as though fate had put me in that seat in front of that computer. I tried to set my eyes on the swirling words. Just a second of following around the bright glare made my head spin. A wave of heat, then a kind of slow thud in my chest like something falling, like a marble candlestick off a mantel hitting the carpeted floor. My heart. "Did you forget something?" The words were twisting across the screen, taunting me. Who had written such a thing? The computer next to me had by then gone black, dead. I thought of the aborted fetus again and felt sick to my stomach. I was probably hungry, my blood sugar low. But I felt very emotional there. I felt a bit like I'd been abandoned in a bad dream. The words swirled by again. My hands began to shake. What was this? What was I forgetting? Magda? Is this you? What a strange responsibility it was, to hold someone's death in your hands. Death seemed fragile, like crumpled paper, a thousand years old. One false move and I could crush it. Death was like old, brittle lace, the appliqué about to separate from the fine mesh threads, nearly shredded, hanging there, beautiful and delicate and about to disintegrate. Life wasn't like that. Life was robust. It was stubborn. Life took so much to ruin. One had to beat it out of the body. Even just the slightest seed of life, a fertilized egg, took payment, an expert, a machine, and an industrial vacuum, I'd heard. Life was persistent. There it was, every day. Each morning it woke me up. It was loud and brash. A bully. A lounge singer in a garish sequin dress. A runaway truck. A jackhammer. A brush fire. A canker sore. Death was different. It was tender, a mystery. What was it, even? Why did anybody have to die? Walter, the Jews, how many innocent children . . . my thoughts lost their train. How did people go on with their lives as though death weren't all around them? There were theories—heaven, hell, rebirth, and so forth. But did anybody really know? Was there an answer? How unfair it seemed to send the living off into death, into the unknown, so cold. Blake must have understood as well what a tragedy this was. It was right there, in his words, **Nobody will ever know who killed her.** Why, God? I'd been too hard on Blake, I thought. Blake had given my poor Magda a place to rest. He'd tried his best with all that he had—a pen, a spiral notebook, the little black rocks, which I now remembered were still in the pocket of my coat. I stuck my hand in and felt them, sharp and gritty between my fingers. They were a comfort. They gave me some strength. **Her name was Magda.** Yes, Blake, we must insist on life, acknowledge it, never turn away from the dead.

I looked back at the computer, stared straight at the swirling taunt from beyond. There was a tiny printed sign laminated and taped along the bottom edge of the computer screen saying the same thing: "Did you forget something? We aren't re-sponsible for lost or stolen objects. Please leave your desk the way you found it." It seemed to me a cruel message: Yes, yes, be alive, make your mess, but when you die, leave not a trace. Sweep up any evidence of your existence. Reminders will only trouble those who live on. They'll have to waste their own lives cleaning up yours. It was like Magda's dead body was some candy-bar wrapper littering the sidewalk.

I felt exhausted by my own thoughts by now. I wished I could just forget all this, go back to my innocent stroll through the birch woods, fuss with myself, berate myself for not taking the rowboat to the island. "Lazy woman," I'd called myself. Oh, I'd go soon. I'd go, I'd go. I'd avoided it, out of laziness, but fear, too. There was something lonely about being out there on the water, I had to admit then, watching the screensaver twist around. I wiped the tears from my face and as I did so, I nudged the mouse with my elbow. The northern lights appeared again. I clicked open the browser and Asked Jeeves, not the answer to my prayers—for there to be no death, for Walter to be here, with me, for me to return to my life back in Monlith, my life before Charlie, before any of this—for I knew no computer could deliver that. No, instead I Asked Jeeves for a way to take action, some help in my effort to make the world a better place, death and all. Walter would have been so proud. "How does one solve a mystery?" I typed. And then, for good measure, I added the word "murder" before "mystery," since this was indeed what I was dealing with.

I scrolled down the search results.

**Make a list of suspects,** one website suggested.

That seemed easy enough to do. If there is a group of people, each of whom have a reason to want Magda dead, would it stand to reason that the person with the best reason would be the murderer? How would I measure and compare their reasons? "Magda stole my hairbrush," one girl might say, just for example. How would theft of property hold up against something more intangible, like a personal affront: "Magda called me a bad name." Or "Magda slept with my boyfriend." Well, that was real motive there. But how would such a motive compare to "Magda slept with my husband"? Was that worse? Surely it all depended on the quality of the love relationship between the suspect and this man Magda had slept with. And also the sanity level of the person whose hairbrush she'd stolen, the fragility of the spurned girlfriend or wife. I couldn't imagine Magda would ever insult anybody, ever sleep with anyone. There was something a little coy about her, sure, a little secretive, a little dark—black chipping nail polish, the letterman jacket worn with some irony, some disdain—but she was not a "whore." She was not a "slut." I imagined the girlfriend or wife calling her such names. Magda was too young to get into all that, mixing herself up with men, making those sorts of messes. Or so I thought.

There was a lot to take into consideration. Resentment seemed hardly enough criteria to motivate a murder. There must be more to it than that. The question one ought to ask was "Who would profit most from Magda's death?" The answer to that could lead, perhaps not directly, but eventually, to the real killer. I felt very smart for having arrived at this question.

As I thought this through, a little window popped up in the lower-right-hand corner of the computer screen. It was an animated advertisement for binoculars. The lenses of the binoculars widened and stretched, like two flaring trumpets. I clicked on it—perhaps stupidly, I was seduced by the animation—and was brought to a page selling hunting gear that camouflaged the wearer according to a variety of backgrounds: military fatigues of all kinds, then full bodysuits of midnight black, head to toe, with masks and netting over the ears, nose, mouth, and eyes. They reminded me of mimes' costumes. I almost giggled, looked down to my right where Charlie usually sits whenever I sat at my table, but of course he was not there. I was sorry he was stuck out in the car, waiting for me. I would make it up to him somehow. The models were all unisex Styrofoam mannequins with neither breasts nor bulges, straight torsos, and sturdy but shapely legs. I clicked through the selection of patterns on the bodysuits. There were suits for disappearing into different forest landscapes: evergreens, deciduous, coniferous, alpine, jungle, summery green and lush, or wintery silver and gray. They had suits for hiding in fields, in deserts, even in water. I clicked on one that seemed appropriate for the pines: dark, with red patches, light pumpkin-colored feet. They were like zip-up pajamas for children, "onesies." It had been a long time since I'd bought anything for myself to wear. I'd lived the whole winter in the same thick gray wool sweater, long underwear, and brown corduroy pants. Now that it was spring, I'd moved into light fleece, cotton knits, blue jeans. I kept myself on a budget, but I could afford to splurge now and then. "I'll skip the donut today," I reasoned, as though that could offset the cost, and decided to order the cheapest suit they offered. It was just plain black. It cost only twenty dollars plus shipping. I thought I could wear it by the water at night, or even in the water, see if the fish would be able to tell I was there, or if they'd bump into me. Maybe I could take up fishing. That could be very fruitful—a hobby that would keep me fed. Along with my new garden, I'd be nearly self-sufficient. These thoughts cheered me up. "Look, Walter, I'm being both frugal and industrious." This was what he'd meant by "how to be alive," wasn't it? To live life to the fullest? Hatch plans, be spontaneous, put yourself out there, come what may? I took my credit card out of my purse and punched in the numbers. It was rare that I ever received any mail. Usually it was the electric bill, but even that was unnecessary: the monthly costs were automatically withdrawn from my bank account. So to order something for delivery felt especially luxurious. I even paid fifteen cents to print out the receipt that popped up, which the librarian handed me, tight lipped, poor woman, she must have been so bored. In all this excitement, I'd forgotten the window beneath the one for the bodysuit website. It was still up there. "How to Solve a Murder Mystery."

I scrolled some more.

**One way of flushing out the guilty suspect is to ask each suspect outright "Why did you murder [victim]?" If the suspect is innocent, he or she might reply "I didn't," while the actual murderer will have to use cunning to avoid detection. You can actually use this as a process of elimination.**

**Base your strategy around finding the liar. Further information can be found . . .** et cetera.

This was very interesting to me. But people lied all the time. It was part of what kept us whole as individuals. A little lying never hurt anybody. It kept the bounds of what one person was distinct from what another person was. Of course, some relationships demanded more honesty than others. A husband and wife, for example, ought to try to tell the truth. Too much lying would make for a troubled shared mindspace. But it simply wasn't true that lying was an indication of guilt. I lied to Charlie all the time. "I'll be right back," I had said when I left him in the car in the library parking lot. Well, that wasn't quite a lie, but it turned out to be. I'd been sitting at that computer nearly thirty minutes by the time I was contemplating all this. So, not every lie was a deception. Sometimes one had to break one's word. And sometimes, a little lie was good. It was healthy. Not everyone wants to hear the whole truth 100 percent of the time. If Walter hadn't lied to me occasionally, we'd have had a very different kind of marriage. It was good to have a few secrets here and there. It kept one interested in herself.

Blake had already answered the question that I would have asked my number one suspect: **Why did you murder Magda?** His reply was right there in the note: **It**

**wasn't me.** According to the internet, the actual murderer would be more cunning in his response. He'd tell more of a story to lead me away from the truth. He'd hide under a fiction. "Funny you should ask about Magda," he'd begin. "Did you know she once loaned me a book about ancient Egypt? The pyramids are such fascinating structures." Oh, he'd prattle on and on for as long as he had to, to avoid the truth. Furthermore, the real killer wouldn't put himself up for suspicion, as Blake had done by writing the note. The real murderer would keep far away from the birch woods. He'd be doing something seemingly innocuous, pretending as though that was all that concerned him. He'd be folding his socks in a laundromat. He'd be watching television, sticking his blood-stained fist into a bag of potato chips, licking the grease and salt off his fingers. He'd be watering a lawn, waving to his neighbors, cleaning his gutters, scraping the mud off his boots, picking his teeth, humming. Or he was at work in a butcher shop, cutting meat with an electric saw, I imagined. Maybe I'd seen him through the glass walls of the meat section at Save-Rite. I never quite appreciated those glass walls. I didn't want to watch an animal being dismembered. That didn't whet my appetite. Or perhaps being a butcher was too violent, too obvious a profession. Someone with a homicidal temperament might want to pass himself off as gentle and harmless, a wolf in sheep's clothing. That would make for a far more interesting mystery, I thought to myself. I thought of Walter, his kind hands calloused only on the middle finger where he held a pen. He was big and strapping—until the cancer whittled him down, of course—but he looked like he couldn't kill a fly. Oh, but he could. He once beat a rat to death with a hammer. He ate his steaks bloody. Men were deceitful that way. Even the most delicate of them had that flair for the primitive. In the hearts of men, all are hunters. All killers, were they not? It was in their blood. And yet they could appear so kind. One could never tell a man's true nature from looks alone. If there was anything I'd learned from Agatha Christie, it was that oftentimes the guilty party is lurking just underneath one's nose. The killer could be working in that very same library, somewhere in the back room, stocking things, out of sight. Let us hope he's not presently strangling the lady librarian, I thought. If he was, the mystery would be solved too easily.

As though she'd heard me, the librarian walked back out just then, proving me wrong. I was relieved, shook my head at my own silliness. But one needed to consider all possibilities. I felt very smart indeed. You see, Vesta, I told myself. In just two seconds flat you eliminated a suspect: the man who works in the back room at the library. And you didn't even have to question him. You can solve the mystery with little more than your own mind.

I waved and smiled at the librarian. She grinned at me falsely.

It had been so long since I'd socialized at all. The winter had been long. And I had no friends, nobody to meet for lunch, to go to the cinema, even to chat to on the phone. I didn't even have a phone. The note Blake had left me in the birch woods was as close as I'd gotten to a social call in a long time. I'd received no welcome pies, no best wishes from my neighbors when I moved in. Only those dreadful policemen who had come to scold me. As if I were some kind of criminal. "That dog licensed?" they had asked. Tyrants. Those cops might get far with bullying, but I would need a subtler, more sophisticated tactic as an investigator. I'd need a more elegant approach, an intelligent method for how to establish—establish?—motive, means, opportunity, whatever else a guilty person had going for him.

A banner now flashed across the screen. "TOP TIPS FOR MYSTERY WRITERS!" I clicked on it. As I expected, the suggestions were all prescriptive, allowing nothing of inspiration, no real creativity, no real fun.

**Reading lots of mysteries is essential.**
That seemed like ridiculous advice. The last thing anyone should do is stuff her head full of other people's ways of doing things. That would take all the fun out.

Does one study children before copulating to produce one? Does one perform a thorough examination of others' feces before rushing to the toilet? Does one go around asking people to recount their dreams before going to sleep? No. Composing a mystery was a creative endeavor, not some calculated procedure. If you know how the story ends, why even begin? Yes, a writer needs some direction, some wisdom and knowledge about the mystery she is writing. Or else she is just twiddling her thumbs, scribbling things down to memorialize her mindspace. It seemed to me that doing so was actually rather humiliating; a sign of arrogance and self-conceit. But I supposed it was indeed the job of the writer to belittle the miracles of this Earth, to separate one question out of the infinite mystery of life and answer it in some sniveling way. Walter had always dismissed fiction as a pedestrian pastime, like television. Agatha Christie movies he supported, however. He found them satisfying, I think, because he could always outsmart me when we watched them together. He brought videos home from the university library. "These are very predictable stories. Don't you see? I can solve it. The killer is always the person just west of center." He talked like that, and I knew exactly what he meant: the killer wasn't directly in front of my face, but within reach. I could always see the answer just as clearly as Walter, of course, but he took such pleasure in being right. He loved to feel brilliant. I had to acquiesce, let him outshine me, to keep the peace. But I knew I was savvy, too. Not an expert at anything, but very capable.

"Use your imagination, Vesta," he would say if I ever looked unhappy. "Nothing is so serious. Cheer up, please."

He liked to tell me that I was the source of my own misery, that I was choosing to believe that my life was limited, boring. He explained that everything was possible, and moreover, everything—every thing and scenario—existed in infinite versions throughout the galaxies and beyond. I knew it was a childish belief, but I had adopted it anyway. Imagining infinite realities made whatever nuisance I had to withstand more tolerable. I was more than myself. There were infinite Vesta Guls out there, simultaneous to me, scrolling down the TOP TIPS FOR MYSTERY WRITERS web page, with only one small variation: one Vesta Gul's hair was falling across her forehead in a different way; one mouse pad was green instead of blue, and so forth. In another dimension, there was a small fire-breathing dragon sitting next to me on the floor. And in another, Charlie was being strangled out in the car by an eighty-foot boa constrictor. And so on. The job of the sleuth was to narrow down potential realities into a single truth. A selected truth. It didn't mean it was the only truth. The actual truth only existed in the past, I believed. It was in the future where things began to get messy.

**Map out exactly how the crime was committed. Imagine every detail.**

This was ridiculous. If I could map out exactly how the crime was committed, there would be no need to solve the mystery. I supposed there were possibilities to consider, there were versions of different pasts that I could list. Then I could deduce which version was most true. That I could do. But "every detail"? How much detail was "every"? Was it enough to say "his beard was thick" or was I expected to explain just how thick, and of what texture, and when the last time the beard had been trimmed, and with what kind of implement, and by whom? If a beard was recently trimmed, would Magda come back to life? No, such careful imagining had to be limited to crucial scenes. If the beard was trimmed in a cave by the quarry in the dark, messily, brutishly, with a switchblade, and that switchblade had slit Magda's throat, then the beard was worth conceiving of. But if the beard belonged to a passerby in Levant with no knowledge of anything whatsoever, then it had no bearing on the mystery. Or maybe I was wrong. If there were infinite universes, with infinitely small discriminating details, then every hair on every beard was of some consequence. Didn't every little thing count? I stared off, considering how I'd ever account for all the beards on Earth, and then on every Earth in the realm of possibilities. But I stopped myself. If there are infinite meanings, there is no meaning.

**Give the murderer a clear and convincing motive.** Well, I needn't give the murderer a motive. The murderer must have done that for himself.

**Create a three-dimensional world. Your characters should have lives that extend beyond the particular situation. You can use the worksheet for writing character profiles to start bringing the characters to life.**

Mystery was an artless genre, that much was obvious. Not that the more literary novels I had borrowed from the library seemed any more inspired. What got put on the library shelves was all the stuff that **won't** surprise you. Blake's invitation, or poem, I could call it, wouldn't have made it onto anybody's nightstand: it was too weird. **Her name was Magda.** What kind of opening was that? An editor would deem the note too dark to publish. Too much too soon, they'd say. Or it wasn't suspenseful enough. Too queer. I tried to remember the openings of the last few books I'd read. I couldn't.

Only one part of the TOP TIPS article seemed useful—the character profile questionnaire. I thought it could help me imagine Magda more precisely. It seemed easy enough to fill in the blanks. That kind of thing was good for people getting older: brain teasers, games. Walter had been keen on such mental exercise. He always had a chessboard set up, and he'd make a move, get up and sit in the opposite chair, make another move. "This way, the psyche confronts itself. There is a dialogue. The mind must be spoken to, Vesta, otherwise it starts to atrophy. It turns to sludge." It made me think of a fountain in the Monlith shopping center, the chlorinated water recycling down and up.

"But if the mind talks to itself," I said, "isn't it just saying what it wants to hear?"

Walter was right about needing someone to talk to. Thank God I had my Charlie. Without him, I feared I might lose all sense.

I took a pen from my purse and began

to write down names of suspects on the back of the receipt for my camouflage bodysuit. This was fun, wasn't it, Walter? My instincts—something the mystery genre writing instructions made no use of—told me I'd need six names. I felt that one must be some sort of monster, some ghoul, some dark, scratchy thing that leapt out of the shadows, a figment of rage representing the dark subconscious of all of mankind. The pine woods were good territory for a character like that. As I wrote the word "ghoul," my hand slipped on the paper and the **u** elided with the **l,** making a single character that resembled the letter **d.** Don't they say that accident is the mother of invention? I could call this ghoul Ghod. He would be rather like a gob of goo and nerves, and I felt very clever in seeing the subtle meaning of the name, so close to God. I was going to be good at this, I thought. But I shouldn't be too confident. An overconfident sleuth could misinterpret evidence. She might only see the clues that would lead her to the solution she'd first had in mind. And

I wanted to be surprised by what I discovered. I wasn't a know-it-all, like Walter. **Try to surprise the reader at the end, but always play fair.** Oh, I'd play fair, but I'd play the game on my terms. I'd follow my own whims and fancies. That was the life I wanted—a free life, free from expectation. That was fair.

I still needed a strong male lead. Someone in his mid- to late forties, a kind of Harrison Ford type. I'd always thought Harrison Ford looked a bit like Walter, handsome, strong, vulnerable, and sensitive, a man with an intuitive sensibility, a mind reader of sorts, someone successful, debonair, distinguished. That kind of man could get away with anything. My Harrison Ford might be an avaricious landlord, making uncouth deals in darkened alleys or the back rooms of jazz clubs, but always with the highest moral agenda, always with a warm heart. And he'd have a posse of good-natured underlings at his beck and call. A staff, so to speak. That might make my cast of characters complicated, to deal with these underlings. So no underlings, I decided. Walter had had only one underling at any one point—young research assistants, all of them young women.

I would call the Harrison Ford character not "Harrison Ford"—it would be hard to separate the real from the imagined—but "Henry." **Regarding Henry** was the perfect point of reference for this character. Someone who had once been ruthless, selfish, a narcissist, but is redeemed through sudden tragedy. He might have lost his fortune, and was now forced to work at the hardware store. Or he just frequented the hardware store in Bethsmane, because he was a plumber, or a contractor, or a carpenter. Anyway, I knew I could find him there.

I had the librarian print out a copy of the character profile questionnaire. She seemed a bit peeved.

I clicked the X's on my internet windows. There were more people in the library now. It was close to lunchtime. I took one last look at myself in the reflection in the dark astral plane of the computer screen. There I was. I was the same as ever, just floating now in the digital abyss like a great seer or a god or just an idea.

I gathered my things, clutching my papers to my chest, and hurried out back to the car. Charlie would be getting cold and sad all alone, I realized.

We didn't stop to walk around in town. I didn't get my usual donut and coffee. We simply sped home, mindful of the Bethsmane police station at the curve in the road around Twelven Creek. I didn't want to bring any attention to myself. I could already sense a shift in the atmosphere. When someone's habits are interrupted, even slightly, a small town feels it and some people might take notice.

Charlie leapt out of the car once we pulled into the gravel drive and I opened the passenger door. He nearly wrenched my shoulder out of its socket, as my arm had somehow twisted around his leash. I didn't think of myself as an old lady, but at my age I am at risk for certain ailments. I'm supposed to—but don't—take my Boniva once a month. It would be easy to swallow it in the morning and walk around for the hour you're meant to walk as the medicine is absorbed into the body. But somehow it felt unnatural, like poison. I didn't trust it. I got the feeling that the chemicals in this medicine would actually leach calcium from my bones. Maybe it was in honor of Walter's dogged dismissal of any fancy pharmaceuticals. When he got cancer, he blamed it on Pepto-Bismol.

For lunch I made fresh coffee, and spread peanut butter on another bagel. I didn't feel like cooking. I took a long hot shower, considering the work I had ahead of me. I had only two suspects so far—Ghod and Henry. By the time I was dressed again, the sun was setting. Time had vanished. I called Charlie back inside.

I hadn't been bored at all that winter. Boredom hadn't even occurred to me. It had been so much work to keep myself and Charlie clean and cozy, to keep the wood-burning stove fed with wood, to clean the ashes, sweep the floors, plug the drafts in the windows with dish towels. Each day I shoveled a trail through the new snow down to the lake, where I walked and let Charlie crunch over the glazed surface. Inside there was hot tea to make, the fire to start up again. Before we knew it, the sun was down and we were exhausted. I could barely drink a glass of wine and open a book before I dozed off on the couch, the dark pines misty with windswept snow, and then it was all dark and the fire gently crackled and Charlie went just a few yards deep to do his business and then bustled back in, and we went up and got into bed, and the day was done. We were like hibernating bears from November to March. April was when things started to thaw. Charlie and I were all right. We had weathered the storms. But now, with Magda's mystery to solve, my winter habits seemed pathetic and mundane. How did I stand to live through all that boredom? How did I not tear my hair out, or start acting crazy, talking to myself, pacing, building friends out of snow? I had Charlie to thank for my sanity, I supposed. When he was sleepy,

I felt sleepy. Drowsiness would fill the mindspace between us. It was like a pill we took in the winter afternoons. A cup of tea, a quick visit to the woods and toilet, and we were out like two melted candles.

Now the days were longer. The sky turned orange and pink. Glorious yellows and violet dashes reflected on the lake. The black trees on my island swayed like marionettes in the wind. I could picture God's hands pulling invisible strings. Maybe Walter was up there with Him in heaven. "When you pass from this Earth, you will know Him," said Pastor Jimmy. I clucked my tongue. It was all nonsense, was it not? What was real was what was down here, on Earth. The world of nature and its miracles, that was God. There was so much joy down here, so much to explore. And there we were, my dog and I, with the lamp casting a warm glow over the table, a hot cup of fresh coffee. I rarely drank coffee at night, but I wanted to be sharp. My usual glass of wine would make me sleepy. I even lit a candle, as I'd often done in the winter, for ambiance. But I lit it now for focus: a burning flame sharpens the mind. This was what Walter did when he was up late working, writing his case studies, doing whatever it was that he did. I turned down the radio, took out my photocopies, lay the receipt for the darkness bodysuit aside, and got to work on my questionnaire.

# Three

**Name: Magda.**

No last name. I liked that she was just **Magda,** a little name floating there in the soft birch woods wind. She was my Magda in that way. I had discovered her. And if the past was certain, and it held a certain truth, Magda's past was mine to discover and know, and I felt I knew her so well already. All I had to do was think.

**Age: 19.**

She was still a girl, I reasoned, but old enough to have a few scars, a few stories.

She had a youthful spirit. Even if she was as old as twenty-four, she would still feel that she was nineteen. And if she'd ever been pregnant, she'd have gone where the couple at the library had gone, to have the baby sucked out of her and ruined and disposed of. She would have no qualms about doing something like that, I thought. Pity, shame. Perhaps her murder was God's retribution. But, oh well. Magda wouldn't want her life ruined with a baby. She wouldn't want to be beholden to a child, or to its father, and have to spend her days spooning up mushed carrots into the face of a creature that was only half hers. The other half, I'd assume, would have been a mistake. She'd run away before she got in too deep. She'd get out of Levant, go south, where there were more people like her, restless, cunning and bold. That was the problem in Levant. Nobody was restless. Everything was set in its ways. Anything that was out of the ordinary was tossed out or ignored. Nobody had bothered to make friends with me on the lake. I had neighbors half a mile around the shoreline. They had waved just once when I passed them in my row-boat. And the way they'd waved was as if to say, "This is our property. Get away, go." I just wanted to explore a bit. I just wanted to know how they kept things up over there. From what I could see, there was a boathouse sinking down on rot-ting wooden pilings, a door locked but hanging downward and open, so I could see inside a bit, but only at the darkness there. And their house, set far back from the water, was hidden by trees. Dark pines. There was a small dock on the property, and that's where the neighbors were, both in bathrobes, standing, look-ing down at the water. They'd seemed surprised to see me, the way the man put a hand out to stop the woman from talk-ing, then pointed in my direction, where I was, twenty yards away on the water. The man was unshaven, the woman had big poofy hair and looked sickly. I waved back, but they turned and walked up the dock and quickly disappeared into their pines. It was odd. I don't think they had any children. On a few occasions I'd seen their big black truck turning off before me on Route 17. If they'd known Magda, they wouldn't have liked her. They didn't like me.

A general physical description of Magda would take some effort. I'd been able to picture her dead body quite easily, and from that I could gather certain unassailable facts. But her face was still obscured.

**General physical description: Attractive, unusual face due to ethnic heritage.**

Some might find it too unusual, especially as it was framed by her long silky black hair that was so slippery, so fine, that it hung on either side of her face like a picture frame. It made her face all the more strange and tender, put on display in such a way. Her skin was pale, but it wasn't freckled or mealy. It was almost rubbery. You couldn't see any pores in it. I imagined that she'd have a slightly upturned nose, a large one. And green eyes? Brown eyes? They were narrow, inscrutable eyes. Green, yes. Berry-red lips when she was living, but now they were pale, white with death, flaky, pressed into the dirt. I pictured her face a bit more clearly from the perspective of the ground beneath it. She wore a lot of makeup on her eyes. Heavy black liner, false lashes, and mascara that made her eyes into tarantulas. She thought it made her look tough. She had a thick chin, a little waddle there that she hated. She thought it made her look fat. She would point to it in front of the mirror at school and say to her girlfriends, "I'm so fat." And she'd flick at the little pouch there. But she was not fat. Far from it. She was a bit taller than the average, five eight, five nine maybe, but stooped down, a posture of both diffidence and revolt. Magda didn't care about popularity. She was more concerned with power in a mystical way, maybe, or in a sexual way. She was feminine, refined, but she was hard. She had a man's kind of intensity.

Manly shoulders, I could imagine. Her fingers were long and there was an elegance about her hands and long fine wrists. She could have played piano. If it weren't for the shoulders, she could have danced in the ballet. But the shoulders were wide because she hunched her back in that way. If she straightened up, she'd be tall and lovely. Perhaps if she'd stayed in Belarus, she'd have worked hard on that posture and would have ended up in Moscow, dancing with the Bolshoi by now, and not dead, facedown and nearly forgotten here in Levant. American children were so lazy. When I saw the little ones dragged through the supermarket in Bethsmane they could barely keep up with their mothers. Most of them sat in the cart, chubby legs pinched by the metal spokes, mouths covered in red from a Popsicle or hands and faces smeared with chocolate. Magda had not been like those children. She hadn't been raised to be a sloth. She was a rebel. She dressed like a tomboy. Her fingernail polish was chipping. She didn't tweeze her eyebrows, but shaved them off completely, then drew them on with brown eyeliner. They were thin, highly arched, odd, punctuating curves.

Every summer, groups of teens from Eastern Europe were shipped over by an employment agency to work the registers in the fast-food restaurants on the main highway, to keep up with all the tourists driving upstate to see the falls or the ocean or parks. They all spoke perfect English, better English than the locals. Perhaps Magda had been one of those fast-food workers, and she'd overstayed her work visa, and had been living off the grid, hiding, working for pennies under the table as a home nurse for some senile old man. This made perfect sense to me. And so it was decided.

**Hometown: Belarus.**

"Times are tough."

Maybe Blake was a friend of Magda's, and he'd convinced his mother to let her

rent a room in their house. He wanted
to help her. Oh, he was in love with her,
maybe. But he was too young for that. He
was only fourteen. He'd barely started
spurting hair in his armpits. He'd never
kissed a girl, poor Blake. But he must
have been a special kind of boy to take
an interest in Magda. He must have understood her situation with the visa, and
that going back home to her family was
far worse than any fate possible in a place
like Bethsmane or Levant. Blake must
have covered for her in certain cases,
with the police, or inquiring higher authorities, the agency that had hired her.
This was why he couldn't make a fuss
about her death. He was protecting her.
She had sworn him to secrecy: "I can't
go back to Belarus. It's awful there. My
father, he is alcoholic. He beats me and
my sisters. Please, help me. Look, I have
money saved from my McDonald's job."
How could Blake refuse?

**Place of residence:
A rented room in Blake's
mother's basement.**

I pictured the house on a back road off
Route 17, just over the Bethsmane line.
A one-story clapboard ranch house, a
dilapidated garage, a field of wild grass,
rusted wire fencing around a small grove
of pines in the back. I knew I was fortunate to have my place on the lake, far
from that kind of trashiness. My property was rustic, certainly. It was fit for
living in, insulated, and when I bought
it I was told that the plumbing could be
improved upon, but I hadn't found that
necessary. The toilet they suggested was
the kind that lit the contents on fire.
They said that would be better for the
environment, since the pipes just emptied into the ground. I'd looked at other
cabins, too, before moving to Levant.
One picture the realtor sent me showed a
badly weathered farmhouse. All the wiring and pipes had been ripped out, and
the roots of a tree were scrambling their

way through the brick half-story founda-
tion around the house. Bethsmane was
poor, and Levant was poorer. I often saw
houses with pine boards over the windows, sheet metal over storm-torn siding, bright blue tarps covering crumbling
roofs. Such was the condition of Blake's
mother's house, I imagined. Perhaps the
bank had been threatening her with foreclosure, and so she'd had no choice but
to allow Magda to rent out the basement,
and keep it a secret. "Don't tell anybody,
or else I'll have to claim it," Blake's mom
said. "Nobody can know she's here."

I had no sense of rental rates in a place
like this. Was one hundred dollars too
much or too little for a basement room
with a bed and dresser in a cheap house
in this kind of nowhere? I had no idea. I
could make an estimate based on what
kind of salary Magda would make, working under the table as a nurse's aide for
the senile old person. That was hard
work, and most people couldn't afford to
hire real professional aides or to live in a
retirement home with constant care. My

guess was that a girl like Magda could be talked into accepting something like six dollars an hour. Six fifty, maybe. If she worked forty hours a week, that gave her two hundred forty dollars. According to Walter, rent should be one's weekly salary. For Magda, as desperate as she'd be, and as desperate as Blake's mother would be to cover the monthly mortgage, which was what—four hundred dollars?—my guess was that she charged the girl two hundred dollars per month to live in the basement, utilities included but no food. Blake might have snuck her down a sandwich every now and then, but Blake's mother wouldn't have liked that. Shirley. I could picture her now, cold eyes but a pleasant manner. She probably worked as a customer service representative, or a telemarketer. There was a call center up in Highland. She'd be good at that. She'd be good at sounding and acting like there was nothing strange or wrong, no problems. Everything was taken care of, everything was wonderful. I was very glad I didn't have a phone.

The basement, where Magda slept and sat around on her afternoons off, and spent weekends alone, huddled under the bedspread, subsisting on snacks from the drugstore—Hershey's chocolate bars, potato chips—was barely what I'd call a "residence." She wasn't residing. It was like she was waiting out a sentence. I felt bad for her. Had I known she'd spent all winter starving and shivering like a blade of grass in the frost, I would have taken her in. From the little I knew of her, I already liked her. We could have kept each other company, and Charlie would have loved her, too, after an initial spate of jealousy. I think she'd have appreciated my kindness. We'd make a home together, stoking the fire, cooking, napping in the afternoons. She could have laid her head on my shoulder and cried, and I would have petted her silky black hair and told her everything would be all right, and then maybe she wouldn't be dead now. Maybe she'd be out there, rowing across the lake, waving to me and smiling, alight in the sunset, her face a beam of golden light, like an angel, like some kind of magic girl. But no, she'd been banished to that basement. It was dark down there, just a bare bulb hanging from a wire, and maybe a little lamp Magda had picked up at a yard sale for a dime, the kind that clamps onto a book so you can read in bed without disturbing your husband. I'd had one of those. Walter didn't like it. He thought I was making a fuss of things, just to get his attention. "If you want to read, read, why do you need to sneak?" He wasn't really angry. He was just pushing my buttons, since I was always so panicky about secrets between us. I was always feeling like he was hiding something from me.

"There was traffic where? And why? Some kind of accident? Describe the car for me. Describe the scene. How light was it when you left your office? You see? You see? I worry. I need to know these things." I would have worried the same way about Magda. I would have been up all night waiting on her, too, if she'd gone out. I would have made a bed

for her on the couch. I never sat on it.
I'd use the roller to get all of Charlie's
hair off, and get her a nice new down-
filled pillow. I bet she never had such
a nice pillow, the poor girl. She was
like Cinderella down in Shirley's basement. It was cruel. She was paying for
this crummy hell, and for what? To stay
out of Belarus? To have freedom here?
That wasn't any kind of freedom, no.
Something awful must have happened
back home for her to want to stay here,
knowing only the highway and the for-
ests, the summer job at McDonald's.
Maybe a few parties, drinking cheap
beer, a skinny-dip, that was all the fun
she'd have here. There wasn't even a rug
on the hard concrete floor of Shirley's
basement, just a few sagging cardboard
boxes of Shirley's dead husband's useless
belongings: an antiquated electric razor,
wide polyester ties, a money clip, shoes
made of fake leather, so tough and sharp
they'd cut your feet. The whole cheap
suit was down there. Shirley was saving
it so Blake would have something to wear

at graduation. Could they be that poor? Is that what life was like? As much as I complained of Walter leaving me alone at night in Monlith, or traveling too much, there was always money. There was always heat, and nice carpets and fluffy towels, food in the fridge, a newspaper on the front step every morning, and I was embraced from time to time. In the winter I had an entire closet full of warm things to wear. And poor Magda, she had nothing. Just those beat-up tennis shoes. Winters were so cold in Levant. Maybe when the temperature dropped below freezing, Magda unearthed the clammy boxes and pulled on the dead man's slacks and jacket to stay warm, huddled back under the blanket, which was probably one of those afghans old ladies knit, pilly and stiff and ugly, and full of holes. Wasn't she miserable down there? Well, Magda was tough. She would insist on enjoying herself. I imagined she had some kind of music equipment, one of those little players with the foam earphones. Maybe she'd listened to the radio, just like I did. To Pastor Jimmy. To public radio. To the bad music on the college station. I imagined she'd rock back and forth on the bed, eat her peanut butter crackers or corn chips, and look up at the small windows just below the low basement ceiling, startled now and then by the loud clank of the oil heater or a flushing toilet, Shirley's heavy feet crossing the living room floor above her. It must have been awful to live in someone else's home that way, like Anne Frank. Horrible, horrible.

Charlie, sensing my distress, rose from the floor where he'd been curled up by my feet and put his head on my knee. "Do you have to potty, Charlie?" Did Shirley's basement even have a toilet? I could imagine that Magda, like some third-world prisoner, did her business in a bucket, and waited for the family to be out of the house before she carried it up the stairs and emptied it into Shirley's toilet. If Magda was as tough and funny as I was imagining, if she was as interesting, she saved a little from that bucket and used it to give that wicked Shirley some pee in her special nonfat milk. Or she dipped Shirley's toothbrush in the pee. A flake of excrement nestled between the bristles. Ha ha! I nearly laughed, picturing the kind of silly revenge she might think up. That was pretty wretched. Where did she get that attitude? Perhaps she'd had a father who liked to make nasty jokes. Maybe she was carrying on the tradition.

This father. I could picture him. He was like my father: of average height, with a thick middle, in a paisley sweater and scarf, big cheeks covered in white whiskers, a beard turning orange from tobacco, always a newspaper in his hand, not for reading, but for carrying around as he paced the neighborhood, as though to appear—when he bumped into a neighbor—that he was on his way to the park to smoke his pipe and read the paper, but he never got to the park. He simply paced and puffed, stopping whoever was on the street with a moment to spare, to discuss things, share news, brag about his children, complain about the state of affairs and so forth. Magda's father was like that, only he always had a dirty joke ready to spring at the last moment. Like all comedians, he was depressive. The funniest people always are. He probably jumped off a bridge or hung himself in the closet. Maybe this was why Magda was so quick to sign up for the summer fast-food job when the representative visited her high school. One more reason not to want to go back home. "My father beat me and my sisters." It was a reasonable lie. Blake would have had more compassion for her if there was an active threat. "My mother does nothing to protect me." Poor Magda. With parents like that, I'd hide in a basement, too.

**Family: Unsupportive.**

Now on to friends. She must have made friends with the other teenagers from Belarus who came over for their McDonald's summer on Route 17. I imagined the organization had them stay in some unused building, maybe a ski chalet up in the mountains, empty for the summer, and got some grizzly local to drive them to work and back in a retired school bus. But that seemed unlikely. And homestays would have required too much checking in, too many waivers, too much that could go wrong with the local families. They may even have just camped outside. The summer months in Levant were ideal for outdoor sleeping. My first nights at the cabin, I'd slept on the couch with the windows open. I'd even thought about dragging out a blanket to the hammock and sleeping under the stars. Perhaps the Belarus McDonald's Staffing Company stashed the teenage workers in the pine woods, in fact, picked them up and dropped them off on the side of the road. They'd be too far away for anyone to come and complain of foreigners, strangers, weird kids. And there was the lake to tempt them. "Come to America, you'll stay in a rustic resort locale, work in a clean American restaurant, practice your English, wear a nice uniform, make friends, have a good time." They could have stumbled upon my little cabin by the lake, had parties, taken shelter from the bugs. There had been no evidence of trespassing. When I moved into the cabin, it was empty but for the old refrigerator, the small table painted Girl Scout green, and the remains of what you might call a mural, little white stencils of girls diving and dancing and shooting bows and arrows. If the teens from Belarus had been there, they'd have had to sleep on the floor. I imagined their mildewed towels drying on the line between the trees, a group of them standing in their old-fashioned underwear, dripping with lake water, staring at the lame, rotted ropes of the old swing. They'd all probably be getting pimples and gaining weight from all the McDonald's they'd been eating. Or maybe they didn't eat any of it. Maybe there was some rule against them eating it. If they had even a French fry, the manager would threaten to send them home.

Magda would have confided in at

least one of those teens: "I'm not going back to Belarus. I will run away. If they look for me, tell them I got on a bus, I took a ride, I went to California, far away. I'm not here." And the day the van came to collect them for the long drive to the airport, back to Belarus, back to high school, now tanned and with a few American dollars in their pockets, Magda was long gone. But why had she stayed in Levant? What kept her here? She could easily have hitchhiked out, even taken a bus with her meager earnings. There must have been something or someone keeping her here. I pictured her now, sitting on the floor of the cabin with her back against the wall in front of me, smoking a cigarette in her letterman jacket, which I knew now she must have bought from the Goodwill in Bethsmane. She'd brought no winter clothes with her from home. She would look at me with a shrug as though to say, "What do you want to know?"

You must have found Blake to be a bit of a nuisance, someone you had to entertain from time to time. Just a child who looked up to you, right, Magda? You allowed him to think that once he was older, the two of you could have some kind of romance?

Another shrug.

Did you send a note back with your friends from Belarus? "Give this to my father."

I heard her voice in my mindspace.

**Don't try to find me. I am very far away and I am never going home. Goodbye forever.**

I couldn't think of what Magda's mother would do when she found out, or what the staffing company would say. Would the Belarus police be involved? Would there be an investigation? A missing person's report? I doubted it. The company would get too much flak. And what did it matter, just one girl? Let her go. Let her have her fun, her life. The mother would probably assume she'd gone off with some rich old man. To hell with Magda, the mother said. I have other daughters. What more could she do? Call a lawyer? Pshhh. Who could fault her for not chasing Magda down? There was the note to point to. **I am never going home. Good-bye.**

**Friends: All back in Belarus.**
One of them must have delivered Magda's note personally to her mother. Slid it under the apartment door.

**Don't try to find me. I am very far away and I am never going home. I am gone. Good-bye.**

I clucked my tongue. Again Charlie put his head on my knee. "Don't worry, little boy. She's in a better place." Silly how I lied to my dog the way one lies to a child to protect it from harsh truths. Heaven was not for me. Pastor Jimmy and his congregants, scattered throughout the land as far as the signal reached, and my Charlie, heaven was for those little gullible souls. Walter was not in heaven. I knew that. He was dead. All that existed of Walter were his ashes. Again, I thought of that urn, how I'd yet failed to take it out in the rowboat and dump the ashes in the lake and be done with it. A chill ran through me thinking of doing it now, in the night, under the dim moon that sat like a clock in the sky. Night had fallen as I'd been writing and thinking. I sipped the coffee, cold and bitter. I read Magda's note again. **Don't try to find me.** Charlie pawed at my leg, hungry. I put down my pen and went to the fridge, my steps creaking loudly in the silent cabin. I looked out onto my garden, imagined the little seeds burrowing for warmth in the ground. Had I planted them correctly? In the fridge the chicken sat, raw and dead, and I didn't feel like roasting it. I opened a can of lentils, poured them into a bowl for Charlie, and set the bowl on the floor. He looked up at me as though I had just kicked him. "I'm sorry," I said, and poured myself a glass of water. It was ice cold, and had a strange acrid taste that reminded me subtly of Walter's aftershave, but I forced myself to drink it. I took an apple back to the table. Charlie followed me, but I pointed at the bowl. "I'll make you chicken tomorrow. Eat the lentils or go to bed hungry."

**Relationship status: Single.**

That was easy. She couldn't have been married, and if she'd had a boyfriend, he wasn't her boyfriend anymore. She was dead, after all. But if she had had a boyfriend while she was alive here in Levant, I imagine it would have been a rather tricky situation. I pictured two lovers, in fact. One young, handsome, supple in personality and body—finely muscled and flexible, I mean—with a strange wide face, but thin, gangly even, not quite filling out his body. Aha, I nodded. Another suspect! His name would be something archaic, but silly. Leo. Leonardo, Magda would call him. He was still a child himself, could offer her nothing but affection and tenderness, sweet kisses. Magda would have been far more mature than him. Oh, this would have made Blake jealous, if he'd known about it. Magda wouldn't want to hurt Blake, so she must have been secretive.

She and her boyfriend would have had a private meeting spot, someplace unlikely and romantic. The birch woods, perhaps? "What are these bruises?" Leo would ask her, kissing her neck like a fawn. That was a very good question.

There must have been another, more brutish kind of lover, someone Magda was indebted to, someone who knew her secret status as a stowaway, a runaway, an illegal immigrant, an absconder, and who used that information like an ax he carried over his shoulder, ready to swing it down on her the moment she refused him. But who would do that? Someone not quite right in the head. He wasn't evil exactly, just sick in love. Desperate to keep Magda near him. Perhaps he was the son of the old man Magda was paid to care for. I could picture it: Magda dutifully wiping down the kitchen table after the old man had eaten his soup, Henry coming home, a live fire burning in his loins after a hard day of work. And he'd come down on Magda, backing her into a corner. And although she'd submit eventually, there was always a debate, a reckoning, a promise that if she didn't put up a fight, he'd pay her the daily wages, let her go, keep mum to authorities. Magda was at his mercy, and yet, somehow, I also got the feeling that Magda enjoyed some part of their arrangement. Perhaps it was only that it gave her freedom: spending money—cash—in her pocket. Maybe just that? I wondered. She could have been the kind of girl to get into the dark and dirty, to relish some kind of painful intimacy, forced not against her will, but by choice, to submit to the man. Perhaps he wasn't as awful as I'm imagining. Perhaps he really was something like Harrison Ford, like Walter. But his disability made it hard for him. And Magda was attracted to that vulnerability. Poor Henry. Poor Magda. I wonder if they made love there on the kitchen table while the old man watched and dribbled drool across the lap of his pants. My goodness.

**Relationship with
men: Complicated.**

**Relationship with
women: Distrustful.**

I couldn't forget about Shirley. I wondered how the woman of the house would regard the girl in the basement. Magda wasn't so pretty as to elicit the kind of resentment grown-up women can have for sexy teens. I'd never been jealous of any young woman's looks. For me, it was like seeing a cute little squirrel. This one has big eyes, that one has a charming stripe, et cetera. But some women really take offense at youth and beauty. Good for Magda, she had only the former. Not that she was unattractive. I think she was very attractive in her attitude. And her skin—creamy white, "snow" white they say, like the fairy tale. For a moment I pictured Magda as Snow White, sweeping my cabin, birds alighting on her shoulders. But Magda wasn't nearly as cheerful. Perhaps that's what saved her from inciting Shirley's resentment: Magda was a sourpuss. Knowing she was down there, knowing that she must be exploiting herself somehow in order to pay for her pathetic little home in the basement, must have inspired a bit of guilt in Shirley. She was a mother, after all. And maybe she didn't like Magda smoking down there. "Go down and tell her I don't want my house to smell like those disgusting cigarettes," she'd tell Blake when he came in for dinner. Shirley would be at the stove, stirring a pot of macaroni, her temper high, cheeks flushed.

"OK, Mom. You want me to tell her now?"

"Well, no, not now. Later. And don't tell her mean. Just tell her it would be better if she did it outside. And tell her it's bad for her health. A girl her age, she's still growing."

Magda scared her. That's it. Magda was a bit scary. She was tough. Her accent was thick. Her voice, low and raspy, made her sound like a hit man. I could imagine her male cousins in Belarus, tall, loping thugs in dull black leather jackets, huge shoulders, ready to whack you with a club if you insulted anyone in the family. Magda would have been like them, had she not been born a girl. My guess was that, for her to want to stay hiding out in Shirley's basement in Levant, cleaning up an old man's spittle and having sexual relations with his son, life back in Belarus must have been pretty awful. Thank God she got out of there. In a huff, I turned the questionnaire over again and reread Magda's note: **Good-bye. Don't try to find me. I am never going home. I am gone.** And even though I knew the note I'd found that morning in the birch woods hadn't gone quite like this, it seemed like the two notes could have been written by the same person. And while Charlie pawed at my ankles, I dared to write a new note.

**My name is Magda,** I wrote. **Nobody will ever know who killed me. It wasn't Blake. Here is my dead body.**

I got up and pulled a throw blanket

from the couch and wrapped it around my shoulders. I was shivering, I realized. I suddenly wished I had a cigarette, though I hadn't smoked in fifty years, not since I'd met Walter and we'd decided to quit together—he his awful cigars, me my cigarettes, which at the time didn't trouble me at all, they were like air, they were like my oxygen. If I smoked one now it would make my head spin. Just a little smoke from the wood-burning stove had me in coughing fits. Maybe I had cancer, I thought. Maybe I was dying, too.

**Here is my dead body,** I thought, sitting back down. Who would find me here, dead in my cabin? Poor Charlie, he'd starve. He'd have to bust out of here somehow, chase down chipmunks. Maybe he'd learn to catch fish in his teeth, though I worried the little bones would catch in his throat and hurt him. Eventually, someone would come by and find me, my skeleton slumped over the table, the note snagged under the bones of my hand. **My name is Magda. Nobody**

**will ever know who killed me.** Charlie stared at me brokenheartedly.

"I'm not dead yet, Charles," I said, petting his head and ruffling his ear. I could hear him swallow, and a pang of guilt forced me up again, holding my pencil between my teeth—like a real writer! I fried three eggs, shoved two of them into Charlie's bowl of lentils, and ate the third myself, off the fork, blowing on it and nibbling it as I went back to my writing table, then swallowing it nearly whole.

I went through the next few questions easily.

**Job: Former fast-food worker. Now home aide.**

**Favorite pastimes: Smoking cigarettes, listening to the radio.**

I wondered whether Magda was the kind of girl who read fashion magazines, who aspired to be rich and famous. Maybe this was part of the great plan to hide out in Shirley's basement. She was saving money, and then she'd get out of there, down to New York City, or out to Las Vegas, or Hollywood. I could picture Magda looking at old travel guides to Miami, Florida, where everybody was tan and wore string bikinis on roller skates, with the palm trees and tacos, everybody friendly, dancing, everything clean and pink and the ocean warm, so inviting.

Why hadn't Walter and I ever gone on a fun summer getaway? Because Walter wasn't much for good times. He liked schedules and work. He felt life was best spent being productive. I agreed with him for the most part when he was around, and I'd had my days free to do what I pleased. I did puzzles, I read some books, I walked through Monlith's shops and things, saying hello to people who knew me. I strolled through the public parks. I was a bit like my own father the way I'd just linger around, waiting for someone to strike up a conversation. But that was Monlith. People were bored, especially the women. Magda would want excitement. She'd want to go to

Miami Beach and meet some billion-
aire on the seashore. I could see her in
a black, glittery, cheap bikini, her skin
white, so white she'd have to wear a big
hat to protect her face. "The body is perfect but the face, it's a little piglet." Well,
I liked Magda's face fine, what I could
see of it, as I imagined it smushed into
the soft birch wood floor. She was just
lovely if you asked me. And any old man
would be lucky to spend even a few minutes in her company. I wondered how
far Magda's scheming went. I wondered,
too, had she'd gone back to Belarus, if
she'd sign up for one of those Russian
bride websites. But then she'd end up
with a short, cross-eyed ex-military factory worker and have to live somewhere
like Idaho. Just picturing the vinyl place
mats and the fake marble countertops of
the kitchen she'd have to sponge down
after making the man fried chicken had
me turning over the questionnaire again.

**Nobody will ever find me.** Good. You
are free, Magda. Nothing bad can happen

to you now. You can't make a single mistake. Everything you do is right.

**Favorite sports: None.**

Not in the way people have favorite sports teams or players here, at least. People, men and boys especially, but some women, too, seemed to ally with sports teams as though it were a matter of personal pride. What had these fatsos done but sit and stare? What had the fatsos contributed, apart from buying the sports drinks and bragging to their friends that their team was the best? Is that really how you show your support? Wave a flag? What was support but a vocalized wish? A hand on a shoulder, at most? When Walter died, a few neighbors and some of Walter's colleagues dropped by the house to offer their support. How was I to take that? Did they think I would call them up to say, "I'm ready for that support you offered, how can you help me?" I didn't know how to ask for what I needed. I didn't even know what I needed. The university had handled the memorial, the interment, the reception. Walter's secretary had called me with several options of urns. Of course, I approved the purchase of the most expensive. She pressured me into it, but I wouldn't have felt good about taking the cheaper one—badly polished steel—or the cheapest, which was just unvarnished pine. But maybe the pine would have been better. Then I could have just left the wooden urn out and let the centipedes eat it. That was more civilized than dumping the ashes out into the water, then rowing back to the shore with the empty brass urn. What would I fill it back up with? Dirt from the garden? Plant a tulip bulb?

**Favorite foods: Pizza. Peaches. Orange soda.**

**Strongest positive personality traits: Resilient. Self-reliant. Manipulative.**

**Strongest negative personality traits: Rude. Secretive.**

**Sense of humor:**

Like her father, Magda found humor in cruelty and stupidity, buffoonery. She poked fun at people who were slow and fat and ugly. She was full of spite and arrogance, and it made her laugh to push someone unpopular down in the mud. Back in Belarus, people had thought she was a bully. But she'd had to be. She'd had to be tough, coming from that kind of family. She wasn't soft and girly. But I think underneath the hardened exterior, under the swagger, the eye-rolling, the flat expression she put on to dissuade interest when she did make an appearance to buy canned soup and candy at the market, she was actually sensitive and tenderhearted. She had to be. Why else would I have liked her? Perhaps I'd even passed her in the grocery store once, and I'd been too concerned with my own feelings of being out of place—I'm old, a stranger, an invader, unwelcome, paranoid from days on end of isolation in my cabin—to notice the other odd one out. Magda in her dirty tennis shoes, long, slippery hair hanging over her face like a sheet, hunched shoulders, carrying her basket of cheap, nonnutritive foods to the checkout, chewing Bazooka gum. In the winter, she must have worn a black knit cap. I could almost remember seeing her in the fluorescent aisles, wondering who would be going around in tennis shoes in such cold weather, no socks. "Kids today." I probably clucked my tongue, and assumed the girl was on drugs, a bad seed. Poor Magda. What she really needed was a soft cushion by the fire, someone's lap to lay her head on. I'd have cooked for her, fed her back to health and serenity. "Go swimming now, Magda, it will be good for you." And we could have joked. We could have laughed at Charlie. Scrabble would have been fun to play with Magda. I'd teach her high-scoring words, and we could laugh at them together. "Exorcize." "Quixotic." "Whizbang." "Maximize."

**Temper: Short.**

Magda couldn't stand people who talked too much. It really drove her crazy. "Dumb American bitch," I can imagine her saying under her breath behind the counter at McDonald's while some teenager gabbing on her cell phone stood there, pointing up at the menu. Having to be anybody's servant must have made Magda furious. She had too much pride to be anyone's slave or mistress. Maybe the senile old man she cared for got the brunt of her temper. "You stupid, ugly old man! You pee on yourself! You smell like caca! Vile dog!" How much would it take for her to hit him, to take some book and bash him on the head? "You cry now? You are like a baby, crying for mama? Everybody must take care of you, because you are so dumb, like a dumb dog, shitting on itself. Pah!"

## Will readers like or dislike this character, and why?

I felt I had gotten to know Magda, and I liked her. The questionnaire had worked. Magda felt real. She had become important to me. We had bonded. I missed her, even. I wished we could have met in real life, even just to shake hands. I wished that she could have seen me so she'd appreciate everything I was doing for her, bringing her back to life in this way, investigating her murder, giving her a voice, **My name was Magda,** so on and so forth. I didn't love her as I loved Charlie, or as I had loved Walter. I loved her the way I loved the little seedlings soon to sprout in my new garden. I loved her the way I loved life, the miracle of growth and things blossoming. I loved her the way I loved the future. The past was over, and there was no love left there. It hurt me to think that Magda was dead, life wrangled out of her body, that she'd been so abandoned, with nobody but maybe Blake to attend to her corpse. It is easy, I thought, to find great affection for victims, emblems of vanished potential. There is nothing more heartbreaking than a squandered opportunity, a missed chance. I knew about stuff like that. I'd been young once. So many dreams had been dashed. But I dashed them myself. I wanted to be safe, whole, have a future of certainty. One makes mistakes when there is confusion between having a future at all and having the future one wants.

# Four

Neither Charlie nor I could sleep that night. It was eerily still out, no wind or rustle, and that late coffee had set my nerves on edge. Charlie, especially, although he'd eaten most of his eggs and lentils, was fussy and kept rising and repositioning himself on the covers. And I'm afraid the lentils must have given him indigestion, since every now and then a pungent aroma crept up toward me, and I had to bury my face in the pillow. My own stomach was rumbling, but I had no appetite. All I could do was try to wait for morning. It was pitch dark for so long. I wasn't scared, exactly. It wasn't that I was imagining monsters or demons creeping through the woods. I knew there were no ax murderers out there. If there was, Charlie would be scratching at the door, howling his head off. And then it would be easy enough to get us both into the car and drive straight out of town. All I'd have to do is put my feet in my slippers, run down the loft stairs, grab my keys, and out we'd go. An ax murderer wouldn't be very quick on his feet, carrying an ax and all. Charlie's warning would give me time enough to collect my coat and purse, even. I wasn't worried that I would be hacked to death, fed to the wolves, even if there were wolves out there, which there weren't. At least none that we'd ever seen. Nor bears. Though there were foxes. But the most they were known to do was break into people's garbage and make a mess. They were no worse than skunks or raccoons or opossums. Still, I'd taken a butcher knife up to bed with me and had slid it under the mattress. Just in case. Because who knew? Who knew? . . . And that was what was keeping me awake— not knowing, and wanting to know.

Where could Magda be, and how had she gotten there?

The questionnaire was all filled out, and I had a growing list of potential suspects. But this did not placate me. There was so much more work to be done. There were people to locate, to question, and how I would do this was unclear. I was not a detective. I had no magnifying glass, no handcuffs. I was a civilian. I was a little old lady, according to most people. I'd have to sneak, I'd have to sniff. I'd have to be a fly on the wall, and overhear what I could, glean, detect things through vibrations. I'd have to use my psychic abilities. Didn't Walter always say I was a witch? Walter would have thought the whole thing obvious. Oh, his constant insistence on spoiling every good murder mystery movie was so much machismo. "It was the pool boy," or "It was the housekeeper," or "He's a homosexual," or "It's all a dream." He really was a spoilsport. But so was I. I did not like tension or suspense. It made me nervous. I'd tear at a stack of napkins, eat a whole package of cookies while I stared at the screen. But I guess I enjoyed that, actually. It made life exciting. I liked fear. "Oh, you're a drama queen," Walter had called me when I picked a fight, usually over money, or how we would spend a weekend. I liked to do out-of-doors things, but Walter was too cosmopolitan. "I will not go **swim** in a lake and have microbes enter up my penis. Would you like that? For me to get some sexual diseases? Do you know what germs are there? It is a cesspool. It isn't for people. People swim in bathtubs. Maybe, if you are careful, a swimming pool. Because it has chlorine, Vesta. Don't you know? My cousin had dysentery his whole life from one sip from a river in Bahl."

"You have it upside down. It's good for you, Walter. It's good to get a little dirty sometime. We can go hiking. I thought you liked hiking. We can go up the mountain. There's a little hotel up there." I was looking at a pamphlet for Dratchkill. "It's not expensive at all. And look, they have room service. No buffet!" Walter hated buffets.

"It is not like in Europe," he said. "It is not the Alps. You'll be with loud pedestrians. There will be ugly people everywhere, shaking their babies up and down. I prefer we go to the city. To a museum. But I suppose you'd like me to take you to Disneyland. We could visit the movie studios, maybe see some hotshots. Your favorite even, Harrison Toyota?"

That was Walter's way of making fun of me. The most adventurous time we had was stopping at a roadside restaurant on the way down to Kessel. Walter got sick from it, insisted I keep my distance from him in bed that night. Just like Charlie, I thought, laughing. Walter could be such a child sometimes. "There, you see? You have it your way. I'm punished for being even a little adventurous. Trying your disgusting guacamole."

But this was Walter at his most German. He was far too civilized. He was a scientist, after all. But that didn't mean he wasn't loving. He was very loving. He'd come from a loving home. His parents, he told me, would renew their wedding vows every night over dinner. He did it with me sometimes, mostly sarcastically. "Vesta, my dear, would you like an ear of corn, and with it, I thee wed," or "Will you take this leg of lamb as a sign of my undying love and holy matrimony, amen?" We'd been married at a courthouse, honeymooned at a fancy hotel in Des Moines, where Walter was working on his dissertation. It was enough for me, I'd thought, but I didn't know what I really deserved. I'd deserved what any nice young lady deserves.

It wasn't warm enough yet to crack the window, and somehow I felt that would be like an invitation to whatever malingering spirit might be outside. Ghod, the black ghost I'd put on my list of suspects, was pacing in the back of my mind. Walter would have thought me foolish to conjure up something so abstract, but that didn't matter. Walter didn't know anything, though I assumed he must know much more now that he was dead. He could be up there somewhere, conversing with Magda. They might even be watching me—Walter with his schnapps, Magda with her orange soda.

What were they saying? I hoped they could see just how smart and courageous I'd been, how industrious, how clever. Walter was probably shaking his head back and forth. "It's quite obvious what the next move must be. Write a note back to Blake. See if he bites. One doesn't go fishing without a pole, Vesta. You were always so wishy-washy. You don't just pray for rain, you drive straight to the reservoir if you're looking for water."

Oh, Walter, I should have dumped you in the lake once and for all, I huffed. It was intolerable in that bed, in the dark with my big farting dog. I needed space. I needed fresh air to breathe. Finally, I raised myself from the bed and cracked the window half an inch. A slot of cold air came through. That was better. I nudged Charlie away. He took offense, stepped off the bed altogether, and curled up at the top of the stairs, stretching his jaws in the near darkness and eyeing me with dramatic hatred. Poor dog. I'll feed him better tomorrow, I told myself. If he was my alarm and bodyguard, he needed to eat right. He needed to be in top condition, especially now, with ax murderers and dead girls and strange invisible creatures limping through the pine woods all night, even if they were just in my imagination.

"Will you be mine?" were the last words I remembered in the morning when I woke up. I'd been dreaming of Walter, his ashes piled around me like an anthill, and then it all turned to quicksand, and someone's hand was reaching out, a diamond en-crusted watch on its bony wrist. The time was ten thirty. I grasped at the fingers, but all I felt was air, and then fur, and from a distance I could hear the clinking of glasses and cutlery on bone china. "**Wilst du be meinen**?" It wasn't Walter's voice exactly, but close enough. When I opened my eyes, there was Charlie, tail wagging ferociously, head nudging my hand, my chin, then his soft, thin tongue lapping my cheek like a warm wet towel.

"Oh, all right, my sweet," I said. I could

feel the lack of rest immediately in my bones, in my eyes, my joints, my feet. I eased myself down the stairs and to the kitchen, laying my eyes firmly on the papers on the table by the windows facing the lake, nearly aflame now with the rising sun. It was late morning. Usually Charlie would wake me predawn, and we'd be up and out the door—my teeth brushed, face washed, and fully dressed—just as the first needles of light were breaking over the horizon. The table, however sunlit, was just as I'd left it. Empty mug, pencil, pen, the questionnaire, and my notebook, which I hadn't used. I was proud of my work. It was as though I were a sculptor, coming down to his studio bleary-eyed after a long night's toiling with his clay; and from the hard work and exhaustion, he'd gone up to bed unaware of the brilliant life-form he'd created and left downstairs to dry, to take to itself in the night, to become a real thing apart from him. And so Magda had become a real thing.

In the kitchen, I opened the door to let Charlie do his initial business, preheated

the oven for the chicken, and bent down
to get a can of nutritional supplement from
under the sink. This was not an ideal source
of nutrition, but I knew I needed one. Walter
was always poking fun at my thinness, comparing me to other women around, at once
humiliating me for being slight, bony, flat-
chested, and them for being fleshy, big-
bosomed hogs. He didn't mean to be cruel.
That was just his sense of humor, a bit like
Magda's. It was hard to have friends without making Walter feel I was conspiring
against him. I think he felt left out: he
could sense most people didn't like him.
"People are idiots" was how he rationalized
his loneliness. Sometimes he complained
that being as intelligent as he was made it
difficult to feel truly accepted. "People are
frightened," he said. "Peasants," he deemed
them. Occasionally he read someone else's
scientific work and claimed to feel comforted that he was "not the only intelligent
being on the planet." What he thought of
my intelligence, I never deigned to ask.
He knew perfectly well why his personality was so displeasing. At the few dinner

parties I gave in Monlith, Walter was on his best behavior. He knew how to impress the people he hoped would fund his research, or a dean who was about to hire a new professor Walter didn't like. In those cases, he could be charming, and acted the perfect husband, holding me around the shoulders, kissing me on the hand in a secretive way to tell me how beautiful the food looked, gracious, handsome, so handsome. A handsome man must be terribly cruel to generate such discomfort in the people around him. Had Walter been ugly, he'd have been despised. The folksy people of Monlith were easily swayed by fancy looks. They were too afraid of seeming prejudiced to be unkind to him. "Walter, the handsome German."

If he was watching me now rinse the mouse droppings out of the sunken rim of a can of vanilla-flavored nutritional drink, he'd knock it from my hand and go to the fridge, take up a stick of butter and a steak, tell me to eat like a grown-up, not like some lazy teenager slurping a milkshake. How nice it was to do what I want.

"Tough times," I recalled the woman at the pound had said, handing me my puppy. I wiped the can with the hem of my pajama shirt and pulled the tab and gulped it down. I could feel the cold stuff filling my stomach. It tasted like malt, familiar to me from childhood. We used to sprinkle it on fresh cheese. Now it was like sludge, but I knew that it was good for me.

I pulled on a pair of corduroy pants and a thin cotton sweater to take Charlie for a walk. I would have preferred to stay indoors and study my papers. But I couldn't let him down once again. I did feel guilty for having kept him hungry, for having shoved him in bed. "I'll make it up to you," didn't I say? He stood in the doorway, his leash in his mouth. "Oh, you can wait one more minute." He sat on the rough doormat and dropped the leash. I didn't brush my teeth or wash my face, but before I went to the door, where my coat was hanging and my boots were sitting, I came back to the table, just to admire my work up close for a moment. Charlie was patient. He didn't whine, but I could hear his breathing get quick and heavy.

**My name was Magda,** I saw in my own writing on the back of Magda's turned-over questionnaire. Without sitting, I picked up the pen and opened my notebook.

**Dear Blake,** I wrote.

But what would I actually write to him? Charlie pawed at the doormat. I ignored him and closed my eyes. The light from the lake came through my lids, turning everything bright red, blood red. I thought of a poem, a line from something I'd heard once, or many times, but not something I'd read, per se. It was like a song lyric in my mind, maybe something Walter used to sing.

**The blood-rimmed tide.**

I wrote that down. And then I felt I had to rhyme the rest, to be proper.

> **Dear Blake.**
> **The blood-rimmed tide, the**
> **sun-lit lake.**
> **I know she died, the hints I take.**

> **To look and find, I seek**
> **to make**
> **The discovery of her body.**
> **Next clue?**

Well, that was an awful poem. I could almost hear Walter groaning. But Blake was just some Levant teen, after all. He'd find it brilliant. He'd think I was a genius. I tore it from my notebook, got my coat and boots on, clipped Charlie to his leash, and off we went, down the gravel path and across the road and up the grassy swell to the birch woods, where it was bright and peaceful. Birds were singing. I let Charlie off his leash to bounce as he pleased. He stopped now and then to sniff, to do his business. Spring was in the air, and I held my silly poem in both hands. It was embarrassing. I hadn't put my name on it. I still had the little black rocks in my coat pocket. It dazed me to think that it was only yesterday that I'd discovered the note from Blake. **Here is her dead body.** Only twenty-four hours since I'd first come to know of Magda. And how quickly we'd gotten to know each other! I read my poem again and again, then tried to forget it, as Charlie and I made our way deeper through the birches along the path, which was just as we'd left it the previous morning.

I kept my eyes peeled for something I might have missed—a drop of blood, a tooth, a finger, one of Magda's dirty tennis shoes. Or oh God, her head tumbling between the trees like a bowling ball. Blake had said **body,** hadn't he? That could have meant headless body. I had to steel myself for that possibility. If Magda's body was headless, surely he'd have mentioned that fact. **I don't know where her head is** or **I didn't take her head.** Blake wasn't a monster, he was just a kid. And a heartbroken kid at that. I wondered how he would explain Magda's absence to Shirley. "Her rent is due tomorrow," she'd say, forking up boxed mashed potatoes, more macaroni, whatever it was those Levant people stuffed themselves with.

"She's probably working overtime," Blake

would say. "To make enough money to pay you. You charge too much, Mom. She works more than you do."

"Don't try to make me feel bad, Blake. If your father hadn't left us, I wouldn't have to charge her at all. Then again, if your father was here, I don't think a girl would be sleeping down there. He wouldn't stand for that. He'd go to the police if he came home to find a stranger down there. And a foreigner on top of it. . . . But haven't I been nice? I took a risk on that girl. I could get in trouble. Kidnapping, they could charge me with kidnapping, couldn't they? She's lucky she has me."

So that was Shirley. Both caring and worried, maternal and selfish. Blake, in his tender pubescence, wouldn't be able to hide his heartbreak for very long. How long, I wondered, until he broke down in tears, spilled his guts, crawled into his mother's bed to be held and rocked. "She's dead!" he'd cry. "I left her body in the woods. But it's not there anymore. She's gone. She's gone forever. No, I don't know who killed her. It wasn't me!"

"Shush, shush now, my boy," Shirley would say. "Just a nightmare. That little slut is just off with some new boyfriend, I bet you."

If this scene was true, if Blake had left the body, and then come back to find it gone, maybe he would come back again, I thought.

When Charlie and I reached the spot on the path in the birch woods where I'd found Blake's first note, we paused. Charlie scratched at the ground, sniffed. Yes, there was something, someone had been here, not us. I could see it in the twitch of Charlie's nose, in his eyes, the soft bend in his ears, not quite pricked like he'd just seen a fox, but curious. Ears attuned to something from the past. An echo. I tried to imagine what he was hearing. Nothing had changed more than would change in a day from wind, from scampering chipmunks, the sun drying and warming the earth, the moon pulling and cooling it. The place was familiar to me now. It had a feeling about it, like something had happened there, a memorial kind of feeling, like when Walter and

I walked the fields at Antietam, following the young man in his silly Confederate soldier costume. "On this spot of ground, so many young men lost their lives, fighting for freedom," or whatever he'd been told to say. There was something that must have happened to the ground once it became a place where someone died, where a living soul took a final breath. It gave me a rush to think of it. I tried to focus on how it felt there in the birch woods. There was a charge, I was certain of it. A magnetized force in the air.

I stopped and took out my poem for Blake. I lay it on the ground and weighted it down with the little black rocks. I placed them in a circle around my carefully penned lines. I wished I had a flower to tuck in, to make it prettier. Those rocks were so harsh, so black, like coal against the white paper.

I stood and watched the soft wind flip about in the shy new grass, the gentle buds in the birch branches like fish poking their heads out of the water. Soon the trees would be full of leaves, and the rushing sound of the wind when it came through would be different. It would be louder. Now it was still quiet, gentle. I could hear the sharp little flipping of the corners of the paper of my note as the wind came and went. Charlie kept by my side. I could tell he was anxious to be home, to eat a proper meal. And so was I. We turned around, and leaving the note there for Blake, I felt I had taken a significant step in my life. When else had I done something so brash or brave or ridiculous?

As we walked back out through the birch woods and down the grassy slope and across the street, I thought not of Magda, but about that line of poetry I'd had stuck in my head. "The blood-rimmed tide." What was it? I had never been one for poetry, had barely studied it, never even considered borrowing a poetry book from the library as my reading. Most days I hardly remembered that poetry existed. It seemed preposterous that there were still poets out there among us. How did they make a living? What use was there in poems, when people had television now? Even a good novel had to compete

with TV shows and movies. I'd seen teenagers at the library watching television on
the screens of their mobile phones. Nobody
in Levant would be reading poems. Not
unless it was for school. The closest school
was in Bethsmane. It was, in fact, just a
block down from the public library. I supposed I could go there and ask, "the blood-
rimmed tide," what poem is that from?
And perhaps it was from no poem. I'd invented it. "I'm a poet," I may discover.

"I'm a poet," I said to Charlie as I rubbed
his head. We trotted together up the gravel
path to the cabin and followed our usual
protocol. I hung his leash and wiped his
paws and opened the door. Hot now from
all the walking, I hung my coat and took
off my boots. The oven was well heated, so
I tore the plastic wrapping off the chicken,
pulled out the bag of giblets, plopped it in
a pan, and stuck it in the oven. No salt, no
pepper or spices. Charlie and I didn't care
about things like that. The giblets I fried
up, with two more eggs for Charlie. And
as he ate that, I took my cold bagel and
coffee back to the breakfast table, to my

papers, my deskscape, I thought of it, and ate and drank and looked out at the water aflame with sunshine. Today was the day, I decided. I would get rid of Walter's ashes. Well, not "get rid" exactly. That wasn't a nice way of putting it.

Charlie finished his breakfast and joined me by the windows. He was very sweet then, belly full, rubbing his head on my lap. He smelled of iron earth and also faintly of feces. I didn't really mind. When two beings live together, the smell of them just becomes the smell of togetherness. I myself needed a bath, but I didn't feel like taking one. It was too much effort to disrobe, wait for the water to heat, address my body for what it was now, so little, just a little thing I had to keep clean, like washing a single dish one uses constantly. I might as well stay dirty, get sweaty on the rowboat, take a bath that night, with my glass of wine. I'd think some more about Magda, make a few more notes. And then I would go to bed and sleep especially well since I'd slept so poorly the night before. In the morning, Charlie and I would go on a big long walk through the birch woods. Wouldn't it be curious to discover my little note as I'd left it on the path there, my little black rocks dotted around my poetic message to Blake? Was he reading it now? I wondered. Was someone else? For a moment I imagined the neighbors had seen me leaving it and were phoning in a complaint of littering. "That weird old lady just left some kind of garbage in the woods. Come out and see. It's some kind of funny writing."

They'd hang up and ask one another, "Is that old lady right in the head? Is she a witch who likes to eat little children?" I didn't trust the neighbors.

My mind wobbled over my poem again and again. "Next clue?"

Charlie was splayed out in a puddle of sun on the carpet. I tried to breathe deeply. I chewed the cold bagel and drank the coffee. The chicken had started to smell, roasting well. It would need an hour to cook. If I left it for a little while, I figured, it wouldn't burn. Nothing bad would happen to it, no. Nothing was keeping me from checking on my poem. Nothing.

And with that, I put my boots and coat back on. I clipped Charlie to his leash and pulled him back down the gravel path and across the road and up the grassy swell and out through the birch woods, following the worn path through the trees until the place where I'd left my note. Though I looked and looked, up and down, far past the place where I'd left it, it was gone. Someone had come and taken it. Even the black rocks were gone. But then I saw them, lined up, certainly not by accident, spelling out the letter **B.**

Well, that was quite enough for me.

"Come on, Charlie!" I yelled, and we scampered out of the woods. It took me less than ten minutes to get home, my heart all ajump and very perturbed by how soon my note had been snatched. Somehow I had been thinking it was all just a game. Blake wasn't real. Nobody was really watching me out there. Everything, everybody, even Magda was just a figment of my imagination. Pastor Jimmy had said, "Sometimes your mind plays tricks on you." But this was no trick. Someone, B, Blake, was out there, communicating with me. And then there was Magda. How was it possible that I'd conjured her up so easily in that questionnaire? It was as though someone had been feeding me the answers, someone in my mindspace had been telling me what to write, as clear as my own thoughts. But how could they be mine exactly? I'd never even met the girl. This made me very nervous, oh, this made me really wonder exactly what was happening, and who was this Blake, and what did he want from me? And how would I do whatever it was I was being asked to do? Could I really solve this little mystery? Find Magda's dead and rotting body? Did I want that? Why couldn't Charlie go do it? He was always sniffing out dead animals and things. Well, I suppose human beings are better at solving the more human mysteries. The body must be hidden someplace Charlie wouldn't go, that I wouldn't go, that nobody would go, unless they were on a mission. "My God," I thought suddenly. "The island."

This was all enough for me to dash inside, turn off the oven, not even wipe Charlie's feet or anything, just grab my purse and keys, lock the door, and get us in the car and drive away. I was panicked. I didn't know where we were going. Charlie was delighted, stuck his head on my shoulder from the backseat, watched the vista through the windshield. We passed the little store with the man with the damaged face. Henry, I thought. There he is. More of the story became clear to me. I could almost map out the entire cast of characters I'd thought up the night before. Henry was the man at the store. There was a little house out back, where his father must live. That's where Magda would go to work, to take care of the old man, and where she and Henry had their relations. Somewhere not too far away would be Blake and Shirley. And then Leonardo. All I couldn't account for yet was Ghod, the ghost creature. Perhaps I'd never have to contend with Ghod. I didn't want to. A chill ran through me as I turned onto Route 17. I was driving very quickly, so quickly, in fact, that I'd forgotten to strap on my safety belt. I did so, and as I buckled myself in, I swerved a bit, and within a second, a police car flashed its lights behind me. There was nobody else on the road. I'd been in no danger, caused no danger for anyone else.

"Sit back," I said to Charlie. I pulled onto the side of the road and patted my hair down. I remembered with horror that I hadn't brushed my teeth or washed my face. There was black dirt under my fingernails. There was probably sleep in my eyes. I may have smelled just as bad as Charlie.

"Mrs. Gool," said the police officer when I rolled down my window. I could see his crotch there at eye level. I could imagine his genitals all squashed up inside those tight black slacks. I squinted up at him, holding a hand over my eyes.

"Gul, yes. How do you do?"

"Well, I'm fine, Mrs. Gool, but you've been driving erratically since I've been following you, about three miles. You didn't see me behind you?"

"I'm afraid I didn't. My dog here must have been blocking my rear view."

"Have you been drinking at all, Mrs. Gool? Take any medications?"

"Medications? None at all. I am sorry if I was speeding. Was I? I'm in a bit of a hurry."

"You were going well above sixty, and the posted speed limit is forty-five. That's over fifteen miles per hour too fast, Mrs. Gool. That's thirty-three point three percent too fast. Where could you be in such a hurry to get to? Do you have an appointment somewhere? Keeping some lucky guy waiting, are you? No, no, don't answer that. Everything OK, Mrs. Gool? Nobody chasing you, is there?"

"Oh, no, nothing like that."

Why was he so curious? What did he know? I could imagine Walter, stuffing his face with popcorn, saying, "It's obvious. He was Magda's lover. He's the obvious killer. It wasn't Henry. It wasn't Leo. Where do you get these dumb ideas? Vesta, look at the evidence. He is angry that you moved into the cabin because he was using it as, how do you call it, a bachelor's pad. For cheating."

Aha, I thought. This is why the cops didn't like me. Considering Walter's theory, I nodded as the officer spoke, pleased that there might be a real reason why he had made me feel so unwelcome when I'd first moved to Levant.

"And there's a blind driveway up there," he was saying. "Who knows when a car might be pulling out? That's why we put up signs. You see?" He pointed off somewhere, but I didn't look. The sun was in my eyes.

"I'm so sorry. Will you ever forgive me?" I hoped my acting came across as truly pitiful. If I could have cried on cue I would have, to prove how naive and weak I was, and to assure him that I knew nothing, suspected nothing. I didn't want any trouble.

"I could write you an official warning, but I think I've made my point," he replied, laying his thick fingers in their black leather glove over the edge of my car window. I tried to smile. "Now slow down," he said. "Hey, buddy," he said to Charlie, his voice suddenly modulated up and breathy. Charlie, my fool, wagged his tail and came forward, as if the gloved hand were going to reach through the open window and pet him. I could picture that gloved hand closing in around Magda's pale, thin throat.

"Mrs. Gool," he said, tipping his cap. I watched in my side mirror as he walked stiffly back to his squad car, which was an odd color for a police car, I thought—blood red. He had a club, a gun. An agent of death. He could be Ghod, in fact, a dark and hungry spirit, an evil ghost. Yes. Ghod. There he was. I'd come face-to-face with him. If anyone was capable of murder, it was Ghod, a life-sucking leach, Satan's soldier. And if anyone knew how to cover up a murder, it was a police officer. I rolled my window back up and waited for Ghod to drive away.

Sitting there in the car, I had a moment of daydream staring into the bright white sunshine. It was like I was back in Monlith driving home from the shopping center, and I was like a little kid for a few seconds, excited for no reason, my mind emptied, waiting at a red light, with no place to go but to go on living and enjoying myself. It was an odd moment to get lost—in the face of evil and conspiracy. But for some reason, I felt energized, peaceful, and young.

Ghod pulled into the road, made a U-turn, and drove back down Route 17 toward Levant. I'd locked my cabin, hadn't I? I couldn't face going into town that day. I felt shaken and vulnerable, as anyone would after a brush with evil. "You're in over your head, Vesta," I could hear Walter say. "Go home. Be who you are. Do a jigsaw puzzle. Water your little garden. Drink some tea."

So I drove home. I thought of the chicken in the oven. I tried to focus on that, and what I could do with it, how I'd carve it and save it—some in the freezer, some in plastic Tupperware in the fridge. I thought of which parts I would keep for myself, which parts I would feed to Charlie. I tried not to think of Magda. I didn't feel strong enough to bring her to justice all by myself. Ghod had sucked the courage out of me. I wasn't even frightened, I was struck dumb. By the time I pulled back up to the cabin, I felt my mind had closed.

Charlie immediately trampled through the pine woods to do his business, then came down the gravel again, thundering past me still on my walk to the front door. He went down and splashed in the lake. I was in a dull, heavy mindspace, but it still made me laugh to watch Charlie play so maniacally, thrashing around the water with a soggy branch between his teeth. The slightest thing delighted him. I wished I could be more like that, and tried to promise myself I'd work harder to be happier. Why was I driving myself mad over Magda? Perhaps I'd imagined the entire thing. It could have been just a bad dream, a fever dream—sometimes it took awhile to get my footing if I'd been sick. I felt my forehead with the back of my hand. Yes, I did feel a bit warm. If I just took a nap, I thought, I'd wake up and everything would be as it was. There was no murder, there was no mystery.

I stopped in my tracks, then, as I approached the cabin door. Something was wrong. It was my garden. It looked different to me. It looked smoothed over, as though someone had come and swept it with their hand and tamped it down somehow. I'd left so many imprints and marks, my boots and hands, my buttocks had even formed two moon-faced hollows in the dirt. And now it was like placid water. It was very strange. Upon closer examination, it seemed that not only had someone swept my dirt, but they'd plucked out the little seeds I'd planted. I dug for them with my fingers, but they were gone. I looked all along the line where I'd planted them, and they had absolutely disappeared. Who would do this? Would a bird peck the seeds out of the dirt? Had its wings produced such a windstorm as to sweep the dirt smooth, as it now appeared? Or was it somebody, some person, who had been so sneaky as to tweeze out my seeds, then used something—a newspaper, or a broom perhaps—to sweep away any trace, any footprints? It was a deranged and evil thing to do. Abortive, I said to myself, cruel, to snatch out the seeds of hope before they'd even had a chance to sprout. I could have cried. And then my sadness turned to spite. Ghod couldn't have had time to do such a thing. Who, then? If it was you, Blake, I thought to myself, I will get you back. Whoever had done it would feel my wrath. I spat at the ground, turned my key in the lock, and went inside, leaving the door open for Charlie, who, probably sensing my displeasure, bounded in with muddy feet, but I didn't care. I turned the oven back on. The smell of roasting chicken filled the cabin, and I let it cook, and uncorked a cold bottle of red wine and went and sat at the table. I turned on the radio. I'd forgotten to put it on when I'd left the cabin in a huff just a little while ago. Stale jazz was all I could tune into. Pastor Jimmy would be on that night. I sat and listened, fuming, my mindspace mostly static and rage, but nothing decisive until half the bottle was gone. The chicken was cooking.

"You stay here," I said to Charlie. His ears horned for a moment. I got up and grabbed Walter's urn off the shelf, held it under my arm as I dragged one wooden oar out the cabin door, shutting Charlie securely inside. By the lake, I righted the rowboat, lugged it down to the water, got in and balanced, and pushed off. It was like taking a cold shower to be out there, watching the world move like a kaleido-scope on the surface of the water. And there was Walter propped between my boots, his fancy urn, like a king's crown or something. I supposed disposing of the urn of ashes would be a symbolic dethroning. I didn't want Walter in my mindspace anymore. I wanted to know things on my own. I'd feel better that way. I could do things according to my own rhythm. I could finally think for myself. I wouldn't row as far as the island that day—if Magda's body was out there, I wanted to be calm and collected when I found it. And so I stopped my rowing about a hundred meters out, held out the urn, saw one last time my dull reflection in the brushed brass, then let it plunk into the water. That was it. It seemed so easy once I'd done it. I didn't say a mournful good-bye. I'd done enough of that already. I picked up the oar and turned the boat around and rowed home.

Perhaps it was my old eyes deceiving me, or my raw nerves still quaking from having found my seeds plucked from the soil, but as I made my way slowly back to shore, Charlie began to bark inside the cabin, and through the few trees that stood between the lake and the windows looking out from my dining table, I thought I saw something move inside. I thought I saw a figure, what kind I couldn't say, pass from the table on one side of the cabin, and backward, to the kitchen. Just a slight shadow whose movement, from such a distance, was nothing more than what could be mistaken for a shifting branch, a blur of wind, a bird crossing from one tree to another, its shape reflected and twisted in the cabin windows. I could have been mistaken, but what I thought I saw was a dark, diaphanous shape—man-size, but only darkness, not a solid body—reading my papers at the table. At first I blamed it on Walter. If I hadn't had to discard him in the lake, I would have been there to guard my papers on the table. I could have blocked that shadow person from getting into the cabin. I could have fought that being off, I could have stood up for myself. That was the sacrifice I'd had to make to be rid of Walter at last. He'd been there to protect me, and so I'd never learned to fight. But now I would, I resolved. Forget being happier, more organized. I would be smart and tough and forge my own way. I didn't even need Charlie, I thought, stunning myself. If I lost Charlie, I'd still be okay. He quit his howling as I got closer, standing on his hind legs to see out through the windows, tail furious. I tied the rowboat to the tree and dragged the oar back into the cabin. Inside, nothing seemed at all different. Upstairs, I saw the empty space left on the bedside table where Walter's urn had been. I quickly rearranged the books and knickknacks to fill the gap. I went down to the kitchen and pulled out the chicken and ate a drumstick, hot as lead, straight from the oven, like I was some kind of animal that had been starving in the wilderness all its life.

I went back to my desk and wrote.

My name is Vesta Gul. If you are reading this, I have been murdered by Ghod. I believe he murdered a girl named Magda, as well. Her body is probably buried on the little island in the lake across from my cabin. Please, feed my dog.

# Five

When I had separated the chicken, wrapped it, and stored it as I'd planned, I fed Charlie and locked him in the cabin. "Be a watch-dog for once. If anyone breaks in, attack." I didn't wait around to hear him whine and putter, I just left and got into my car and drove back to the library, where I felt there was more research to be done. I wanted to go back on the internet. The computer had guided me this far, hadn't it? It was like an oracle, a guiding force. Every detective had some special source of wisdom, didn't he? The computer was like my mindspace. I didn't have the answers, but I had the right questions, I believed.

I drove very carefully now on Route 17. I didn't want Ghod to stop me again. That would only delay the story. I was often tempted to abandon books if they flailed along too slowly. The muddy middle, a reviewer had called it one day on the radio. But if Ghod were to kill me, I reasoned, there could be some satisfaction in coming to Magda's same violent conclusion. She had been strangled, that I knew. A boy's hands, like Blake's, couldn't have done such a thing. It takes great strength to strangle someone to death. Magda was drunk, or drugged, when it happened, and caught off guard. She could have fought the killer off, I bet, had she been sober, awake, prepared. She was feisty like a cat. She had those long fingernails. Her affect was flat, but in a flash she was rabid, furious. She could scratch your eyes out, she could stomp on your heart with her worn tennis shoes. The horror, to think that so much life and energy had been strangled out by those cruel, gloved hands. If those hands ever came after me, I would stab them, I imagined. I would take Magda's switchblade and cut off each of their fingers. With that, she and I would triumph. Wouldn't that be something? Magda's soul would be free to fly up to wherever it wanted. Or maybe it would go into the computer, I imagined, almost laughing to myself. Everything existed on the internet. It was infinity on Earth. It was like heaven. Maybe Magda was already there.

When I passed by the curve in the road where Ghod had pointed out the blind turn, I slowed and peered down the long drive to the neighbors' house. I'd seen them come and go so rarely. They'd been downright cold when I saw them from the rowboat that day last summer, had ignored me whenever we passed each other on the road. It was like I didn't exist to them, I was invisible. But actually, it was more like they thought I was beneath them. I didn't like that. I didn't like them. Passing by the turnout where Ghod had pulled me over, I cringed. I could swear I caught a scent of sulfur hanging in the air, the smell of the devil, that putrid creature, a goblin, an angel of pain and darkness. It was exciting to feel so much spite for somebody. It inspired me; I almost felt like dancing. If I was an artist, I thought, I would paint a huge black-and-red canvas, stabbing with my brush in a frenzy until I fell down on the floor in a heap, sweating and dizzy, the world spinning above me. I wished I could be breathless like that, and for so long I'd believed I couldn't. I was old, I'd thought. Ecstasy was no longer a possibility. All I had left was contentment and equanimity, I'd believed. I blamed Walter for making me think all that. It was he who had no capacity for ecstasy, he who was so frightened of joy and freedom. He was the one who selected the house in Monlith, distant from the world, a farmhouse adrift in vacant acres of grasses good for nothing, not even cows to graze on it. Dry dirt. Crabgrass it was, always that steady buzz of some ugly bug hiding between the blades. I couldn't even picnic out there. Walter wouldn't let me. It was like he'd been my captor. I'd been held hostage all this time, I thought. Now I'd let loose. I'd let myself go.

By the time I arrived at the library, I was again ravenous. I bought a Snickers bar from the vending machine by the door and swallowed it in three big chunks.

I'd never been to the library so late in the day before, and was a bit frustrated to discover that the half a dozen computers in the reading room were occupied by as many youngsters in hooded sweatshirts and jeans so baggy that even the pudgiest of them seemed to me like a little stick figure draped in cloth. They looked like Benedictine monks sitting there tapping at their keyboards, faces wan in the cold blue glare off their screens. I stood and watched them impatiently. Each of them was agape, mesmerized. I could see that they were connected to something that had immense power over them. This was what happened when the mindspace was the internet, I thought. One loses one's sense of self. One's mind can go anywhere. And at the same time, the mind becomes lame when it is connected to something so consuming. Like Walter's ashes in the urn, their computers were containers for these young minds. If I was on the internet, too, I'd just turn into one of them. My mind would connect with theirs. And I didn't want to share my mindspace with these drones. Even the girls seemed like stooges, huddled over the keyboards as though nothing else existed. They had no idea that someone older, someone whose work was far more important, was standing there, waiting.

Was one of these trolls my Blake? I wondered. Somehow it didn't seem possible. I couldn't picture him in the mundane bounds of a world such as that library. I imagined him more like the teens of my day—supple and unweathered on the outside, but with angry or sad eyes, wearing clothes that fit, eager to please his parents. He was beleaguered not by the pressure of what was on the television or computer, but by a desire to succeed and get away from all that. To follow in more noble footsteps, and look for glory in the long term, not short, like these kids in front of me. What were they even doing in the library? Not touching any of the books, that was obvious.

Blake wouldn't be using a computer at all, if he was here. He'd be waiting for me in the stacks, so that's where I wandered, to the back of the library where the books were kept, a room with linoleum floors and beige metal shelves. Strange that the renovations to the library didn't extend to the stacks. Apparently the funding hadn't reached that area. The lighting was dim, and as I walked slowly up the aisle, it seemed I was alone. A powerful stench struck me suddenly, and when I stopped walking, I could hear a soft shuffle, so I looked around the corner of the aisle. It was an old woman, like me, but grizzled, in a long beige raincoat and soiled slippers. From twenty paces she reeked of rotting fish. I hadn't ever thought there'd be homeless people in Bethsmane, but this human was certainly destitute. Maybe she wasn't homeless, but lived in a hovel, some hole in the ground, and trudged into town every now and then to pick up books. I didn't even want to know what she might be reading, which books she might have touched, as though that information would poison my mind against all books, would turn my stomach in some deeper way than the smell already had. My eyes started to water.

"Kids today," the woman said suddenly, stopping and bending over. She picked a book up off the floor, moving so slowly that I wondered at first if she was going to lie down and die. But she dusted the book off and slid it onto a shelf, then shuffled onward. I waited at the end of the aisle until she'd disappeared, though I could hear her rhythmic footsteps, the rustling of her big coat. The stench of her lingered. I inhaled and gagged. For some reason it pleased me to be so displeased by her perverse aroma. My face was in an exaggerated frown, I realized, and had been for long enough that my cheeks started to hurt. I tried to relax and breathe through my mouth. Then I walked up the aisle, as the woman had done, and inspected the book she'd picked up off the floor. To my astonishment, it was **The Collected Works of William Blake.** Blake. Blake. Holding it in my hands, I stood perplexed there for at least a minute. What on Earth was happening? I looked down at the worn red cloth cover, holding the book like a relic, like some charged thing. I turned to the frontispiece. The contents were all in old-fashioned type. It was like looking at a Bible as I flipped through. I didn't know where to rest my eyes in all that language piled up—I didn't know what it meant. And then I arrived at a page where it seemed the spine had been broken, since the pages stopped flipping as though someone's finger had interjected and pointed and a voice in my head said, "Here."

There, underlined at the top of the page, was a short poem, only a dozen lines altogether, called "The Voice of the Ancient Bard":

**How many have fallen there!**
**They stumble all night over**
**bones of the dead,**

**And feel they know not what**
**but care,**
**And wish to lead others, when**
**they should be led.**

It was clearly a message to me, from young Blake, my Blake. How sweet to send me a poem in return. He must have appreciated the poem I had left him that morning in the birch woods. What a special boy he was indeed. And with this in mind, I did something I never would have done before: I ripped the page from the book and tucked the thick volume between the encyclopedias, where I had drifted somehow as I'd read. I didn't care if the smelly woman knew I'd done such a thing. She was some kind of siren, I thought, her strange look and atrocious smell mere flags for me to stop and look. Oh, what joy I felt in finding my next clue, though I couldn't really make heads or tails of it.

It was nearing five o'clock then, and the librarian clanged a bell—how old-fashioned, I thought—and announced that the library would be closing in half an hour. I folded Blake's poem and stuck it in my coat pocket. I wanted to study the poem with my mindspace clear, away from the lamebrained people of Bethsmane. On my way out, I stopped in the ladies' room, which was down a darkened corridor by the back exit of the library. I had used it several times before. It reminded me of the bathrooms of my public school days, the clouded polished metal that stood for an approximation of a mirror, the tight, graying octagonal tiles, the crafted and finely molded wooden doors and panels separating the old white porcelain toilets with jet-black seats. The toilets flushed with such power it was as if they'd been intended to do something other than just eliminate human waste—to disturb the pressure of the air in a room, to suck out some of the energy, to wash out one's mindspace even, I thought to myself.

"Goddammit," I heard a voice say as the flushing ebbed. It was a woman, of course, and when I bent down to look under the stall door, I saw something one rarely saw in places like Bethsmane: feet in conservative one-inch-heeled shoes and flesh-colored stockings. It was not something people did around there, wear shoes or hose like that. Women in Bethsmane wore jeans, or leggings, or sweats. You might see young girls in short pants or miniskirts, but grown women did not dress in skirts or dresses. Bethsmane wasn't for ladies. It was for people who hunted or drove trucks. It wasn't an elegant place. The only wine I could ever find was in the grocery store, and the selection was all domestic. There was a reason I bought bagels that came pre-sliced and needed refrigeration. The bakery where I bought my weekly donut sold bread, but it was mealy and full of sugar. I think they used the same dough for the bread as they did for the donuts. The place wasn't cultured by any measure. People ate fast food. If they cooked, they weren't eating many vegetables. I don't know why, since there were farms all around downstate from us. It wasn't like the ground wasn't fertile. My seeds would have grown had they not been stolen. Women mostly dressed in cheap synthetic materials. The blouses they wore were tie-dyed and glittery, and many women had tattoos on their arms. The more "stylish" women looked like they should be on the back of a motorcycle. The softer types, the ones who just seemed practical, dressed in comfort clothes—tennis shoes or rubber flats you found at the drugstore, even in winter, it seemed. I had proper snow boots myself. I owned a pair of tennis shoes, but preferred sandals in warmer weather, or my leather walking shoes. I was practical, too, by the time I got to Levant, but I had dressed like a lady when I was one, when I was married, in Monlith. I'd worn things that buttoned up and skirts that flowed. So I felt I understood the kind of woman to wear closed-toed pumps and stockings like the woman in the bathroom stall beside mine. There her feet were, bulging out of brown snakeskin, scuffed and worn around the blocky heels. Her ankles were swollen, and the space between her feet was large. She had taken a wide stance, but why?

"Goddammit." The feet came together, clomped across the tile, then widened, and then there was a little grunt. And "Excuse me?" I heard the voice say after a moment.

"Hello? Yes? Are you talking to me?"

"Yeah," the voice said. "Do you see a set of keys in there?"

Instinctively I peered down into the toilet, which I had just flushed. I didn't think I had seen any keys in there when I'd sat down. But it wasn't my habit to check for things in toilets. Even after I made my business, I didn't look. Because why would I? Who would expect to be surprised by a set of keys in the toilet bowl? Who would expect anything to be in there at all, except for what you'd know to be? "No, I'm sorry. There's nothing here."

"Not behind the toilet bowl, not on the toilet paper thing?" the voice asked.

I pulled up my pants, clutched my purse, and bent over. "No, there is nothing in here," I said. I didn't like how close my face had come to that black toilet seat.

I opened the stall door. The woman was large, but not obese like the fat ones. She was only chubby. From behind she reminded me of a clapping seal, the way her buttocks flattened, her hands raised as if in prayer at her chest. She leaned against one of the two sinks there. The blur of her reflection in the fake mirror was white and red. Her hair was dyed and coiffed with hair spray. It was not a nice head of hair, but it was clear that attention had been paid to it, as had the selection of the floral print dress—pastel watercolor pansies on a pale blue background. She had almost no waist, and wore a tight white cardigan sweater, pilly and stretched across the back, wrinkling at the armpits. She was oddly flat-chested for someone overweight, I thought. Her chins were buoyant, but not completely shameful. Her face, when she turned to me, was pale with powder. A clear navy-blue line of makeup covered each eyelid. From where I stood, I could see the widened pores around her nose, the remnants of some pearly shimmering lipstick. She must work as a receptionist, I thought. She must do something in front of people, to be in Bethsmane and make such a fuss about her appearance. Not that there would have been anything out of the ordinary if we were in a normal suburb, anywhere remotely civilized. She'd be a dud in any real city. But she had put in some effort, which was remarkable.

Funny to me that of all days to run into such a person, I'd be dressed so poorly. To anyone in Bethsmane, I was not out of fashion. My worst attire was better than what most people wore to work. This woman had on large fake pearl earrings, as well. She was probably around forty years old, but could have been younger. It was impossible to tell with poorer people how old they were.

"Goddammit," the woman said, her small pink lips trembling in a way that was to me surprisingly endearing. I took a step back into the stall. "I lost my keys," she said frowning. And then she turned away and began to cry. I'd never seen such a thing. I watched her thick ankles as she went to the paper towel dispenser and cranked it. She tore off some of the rough brown paper and blew her nose.

"Are you all right?" I asked her. What else could I say? I went to the sink but didn't wash my hands. I was clutching my purse too tightly. I didn't know what to do.

"It's been one of those days," the woman said. "I come to return a book and now I can't drive home. I probably locked them in the car. Oh, God!" She blew her nose again. "And my son is probably home from school." She looked up at me then, and within the desperation, I could see Blake in her face.

"Shirley?" I said, then dropped my purse. My hands turned numb and I bent over mumbling, "Surely, surely they're around here somewhere."

"Well," Shirley said. She leaned over the sink, her soft body indenting where the porcelain pushed against her middle, her thighs, it was hard to detect what started and ended where under that confusing floral pattern. "I don't know what to do now. I have an extra car key at home, but it's ten miles from here. Do you know . . . ?" And her voice trailed off. She licked her finger and swiped the rim of her lower eyelid, then wiped the black stuff that came off— mascara—on the paper towel. She blew her nose again. From her pocketbook she pulled out a tube of lipstick and dabbed it on, staring into her vague reflection in the polished metal.

"Do I what?" I asked. "What do I know?" I picked up my own purse, rummaged through it as though it would explain something to me. Blake's poem in my pocket felt like a ticket to something I was running late to. I had wanted to get home, light a candle, decipher it line by line. But here was Shirley, one of my characters. I'd have to be inquisitive, get her to expose herself in a way that would arouse no suspicion. I'd have to get her to warm to me. She seemed soft, overtly so. Standing beside her, me so skinny and ravenous under my down-filled coat, cold in the dim bathroom and tile, I almost wanted her to embrace me, put her arms around me. She was maternal in this sense. Still, I couldn't get really close to her. She might be in on the murder somehow. I hated the thought of that, but women killed children all the time. They're the closest to them and suffer the most having to raise them up.

"I was just going to ask," Shirley turned to me now—she didn't seem to fear me, but she was shy, she blushed—"if you know if there's a bus out to Woodlawn Avenue, out that way? I know there's a school bus. But . . ."

"Did you retrace your steps? Whenever I can't find something, I try to remember—what did I do when I first walked in? Did I hang up my coat? Did I open the fridge? Did I drink a glass of water? Did you think it through? Couldn't you call a cab?"

Shirley sighed. She thumbed through her pocketbook again.

"My money is in the car. My wallet. Probably next to my keys." I can't say exactly how I understood the pretense of this statement, but I took it somehow to be Blake pulling at the strings of fortune.

It didn't matter whether Shirley was telling the truth or not. Blake wanted me to see the house where he lived with Shirley, and where Magda had spent so many months in the basement. He was the one who had taken Shirley's keys and wallet, of course. Shirley may have been in on it, too. I wasn't sure how wide the scope of the scheme was, whether Shirley was smart or stupid. She did seem sincerely upset, but maybe she was just a good actress. A woman like that might have to be, and she was wearing quite a costume.

"I can drive you," I said, "if you show me where to go." Perhaps this was part of Blake's clue: **They stumble all night over bones of the dead, And feel they know not what but care, And wish to lead others, when they should be led.**

I led Shirley out to my car in the lot behind the library. She politely directed me to the house, pointing where to turn, where to slow, where Woodlawn Road becomes Woodlawn Avenue. A boy appeared now in the graying early evening by the side of the road straddling a bicycle, his dark plaid flannel shirt floating behind him in the wind like a cape. He was exactly as I'd hoped he'd be: his eyes were alert but distant, the skin around them almost orange, like healing bruises. His forehead was thick and crested over his eyes, though his eyebrows were sparse, his skin an ashy olive tone. His chin, so unlike his mother's, was cut as if by a knife, chiseled, sharp, and his mouth was wide and thin, his jaw a swooping thing that made me think of a ship's anchor. He'd stopped at the edge of the driveway—two dark, worn, dirt galleys with fresh baby grass growing in a bed between them.

"My son," said Shirley. "Say hello to Mrs. Gool," she said. I'd told her my name when she'd asked me in the parking lot. "Vesta, is that short for something?" she had asked. "It's pretty. Reminds me of Velveeta. Or holy vestments."

"Hello," I said, nervous for the boy to see my face. He leaned over with his hands gripping the handlebars, trundled back and forth like he was revving an engine. His T-shirt was white, his hair short and combed with grease. He wore blue jeans, not too baggy, and heavy black boots with thick, tracked soles. He just nodded at me.

"House open?"

"Yeah. Car break down?" he said. His voice was low, secretive, and caring.

"Lost my keys, so Mrs. Gool gave me a ride."

"I could have brought you the spare," he said, already up and balancing on his bike, ready to fly away.

"Hop in," I called out after him, but he was gone down the road already. "The bike would fit in the back," I said.

"He's probably going to a friend's house," Shirley said. We drove on toward the house. "This is it," Shirley said as we pulled up. "Now let me just run in and get the spare. You really don't mind waiting? Do you want to come inside?"

Of course, this was the proposition I was waiting for, but suddenly I felt my curiosity wane. "Oh no," I said. "I don't want to impose."

"You wouldn't be imposing."

"I couldn't," I said.

"All right, have it your way," said Shirley, suddenly curt as she heaved herself up out of the car and shut the door behind her. The exterior of the house was worn, but more charming than the aluminum-sided box I'd imagined: chipping blue paint on old wooden siding, darkened windows with peeling white frames, some kind of twisting crystal hanging, bewitching things through the small glass porthole window in the front door, which was hooded in a half eave made of corrugated metal. The front steps were low, only two of them, and poured from the old kind of cement concrete that had pebbles pressed into it. I watched Shirley daintily step toward the front door. She did some strange ritual with the doorknob, pulling up then pulling toward her, then cranking her hand back and shoving the door with her shoulder. It opened into a dim wallpapered room and I could see stairs winding down. The way to the basement would be through a door at the bottom of those stairs, I thought to myself. Shirley turned around, her face flush with stress.

"Are you sure you don't want to come in?" she called out to me. "I feel bad. Come have a glass of water, at least, Mrs. Gool?" She waved, holding the door open.

I conceded. I wanted to see the inside of the house. She was a gentle woman. I knew that she hadn't killed anyone, could never. She may even be concerned for Magda, wondering why she hadn't come home the last two nights. Shirley was well intentioned. She was an honest person. A homemaker. The floors in her house were bare and worn through so that the shellac went dull everywhere but around the edges of the rooms and the halls.

"You probably don't want to take off your coat, it's drafty in here," Shirley said, setting down her pocketbook on a white wicker table in that wallpapered front hall. The wallpaper itself was not dissimilar to the print of Shirley's dress: yellow and blue flowers on a grayish background, painterly, not unattractive, but mottled where it seemed there had been a leak down one wall, and peeling in other spots near the ceiling, which had raw plywood over half of it. A pipe had burst, I deduced. There was messy popcorn spackle on the other half of the ceiling. "Come into the kitchen and sit down while I . . ." Shirley's voice trailed off.

"What a lovely home," I said. The kitchen was like from another time, a time I had lived through but had never actually witnessed firsthand, I'd been too well off with Walter. Things were puce green, plastic, fake wood paneling on the kitchen walls, black iron pulls on the drawers, the scent of bacon fat heavy in the frigid air.

"Well, I try to keep it clean, at least," Shirley said, riffling through a drawer in the back of the kitchen.

"Old house like this, must be quite a challenge. But so nice," I said. "How many floors?"

"Bedrooms are upstairs, and the bathroom. You need to go?"

"No, no, I was just asking. It's only you and your son?"

"Yeah, my boy, my little man. He's a good one. He keeps his mama happy."

If she knew that Magda was dead, it certainly didn't seem like it. But what was making her so scatterbrained and emotional? Blake certainly seemed morose outside on the bike, and had wholly ignored me. Wise, I supposed. He wouldn't want his mother to find out about our secret correspondence about Magda in the woods. The stairs down to the basement were narrow, right next to the refrigerator. At the bottom, the door was closed. Shirley wasn't going to tell me she had a tenant. Even if she trusted me not to tell anyone, she'd think I'd have judged her. She'd fear renting out a basement sounded too lowbrow. She'd asked me in the car where I lived. "By Lake David," I'd said. "Right on the shore, in the old Girl Scout camp."

"You're kidding. You know, I went there when I was little. Got awful poison ivy running through those woods. They had little lean-tos out there, for I don't know what. What did you say your name was, Vestina?"

Now she was washing her hands, the spare car key on the counter by the sink. I looked around for clues. It was rude to snoop, but Shirley's back was turned.

"Do you get any flooding?" I thought to ask. "When it rains. Does your basement flood?"

Her face wasn't visible, but she gave just a slight indication of surprise. "The basement," she said. "No, I don't think we got any floods."

Under a collapsible stool by the telephone, I saw something yellow. I took a silent step toward it and bent down. It was the handle of a hairbrush. In a flash, I snatched it and hid the brush in my deep coat pocket.

"I don't go down to the basement much," Shirley was saying.

"I see," I said. She filled a glass of water from the tap. I held up my hand to refuse.

"No? Okay. Well, we can go now. I don't know how to thank you for all this. I don't know what I would have done."

I followed her back out the front door.

"Your son would have come to the rescue."

"But it's not safe to ride bikes out there late at night. Who knows what could happen. The way people drive sometimes . . ."

It was true. I myself had terrible night vision. Things got grainy and blurred for me in the dark. Walter had forbidden me to go out after he got home from work.

"It's true, and the streetlamps, they're too far apart. At night I can barely even see the road. Just the headlights," I said as we walked back to the car.

"Makes me sick with worry," Shirley said, shutting the car door. "But that's the price we pay to live somewhere so beautiful. I hate cities. I went down to St. Viceroy last summer and it took me weeks to get over it, all that noise. Such close quarters."

"But cities can be fun," I said. Now we were driving out into the sunset, back toward Bethsmane. "So much energy."

"I like it here. Nobody bothers you."

"There is that," I said. "I like it here, too. I don't mean to say I don't. I'm very happy."

"Do you live all by yourself out there,

at the camp? I haven't been there in decades. I can't believe it's still standing, if you ask me."

"Yes, I am alone. The structure is very stable. It's actually quite nice. Rustic, but comfortable."

"All us girls went there during the summers," Shirley said. "All the things we did. I wish I had a daughter sometimes."

"Oh, me, too," I agreed. But I just said it to be agreeable. I didn't really mean it.

"Boys are so rough and tumble. Blake puts up with me, wanting pretty things. He's not that tough. And thank God. What they're saying about football these days, the brain damage? I'd rather my son be one of the gays than a total vegetable. Those poor parents."

"That's nice," I said.

"I'm talking your ear off," Shirley said.

"Don't be silly. A lonely old lady like me? It's a pleasure to have some company once in a while. The only person I talk to at home is my dog." As soon as I said it, I became panicked. I'd left Charlie all alone through the entire afternoon. I don't think we'd ever been apart that long, not since I got him.

"You should get out more," Shirley said gently. "I know there's a senior bingo night at Sisters of Mercy. My dad used to go, before he passed."

I drove a bit faster. Shirley made a few more suggestions—knitting circle, book club, volunteering. I could even call on her if I got lonely, she told me.

"You're very sweet," I said. She was.

Why was I so scared of asking about Magda? What's the worst she could do? Jump out of the moving car? Shirley sighed as we turned onto Main Road.

"May I ask you something?" I ventured. I kept my hands steady on the wheel, tried not to tense up or shake, although I was nervous. I felt Magda's hairbrush inside my coat pocket. The handle of it was like a gun I could pull. It calmed me.

"Well, yes, Vesta, of course. How can I help you?" Shirley sounded like a customer service agent at the power company. Every time I'd called them in Monlith, they sounded just like that—chipper, happier than a normal person should be.

"Have you ever heard of any strange crimes around here, in the Levant area, or in Bethsmane?"

"Oh, honey, you know these fools are fiddling with drugs around here. Two summers ago a trailer over on Brooksvale blew up. Exploded. You see people high as kites wandering around these parts. They'll use any old place to cook their drugs."

"No dead bodies?"

"Well," she paused, and pinched her lips as she thought up her answer. "People die all the time, don't they? Sad as it is, life is short, bless us all. Isn't that right?"

"But no murders, then?"

"You sound just like my son. Boys his age are fascinated by that gruesome stuff."

"Your son is?"

"You know, we need to keep an eye on our youngsters, with all the violence in this world. I don't know where they get those twisted ideas. From movies, I guess."

"From computers."

"Lord knows."

"So no murders?"

"Not that I've heard." She was turned toward me in her seat, pulling the seat belt away from her bosom. "Are you afraid out there alone in that old cabin? Reading too many scary books?"

"That's what it is. My head's just filled with scary stories."

"Read something nice tonight, sweetheart," she said. "Something to set your heart at ease. Nobody's going to come after you, Vesta, don't worry. You hear anything funny going on, just ring up the police. They'll come out right away. But I'm sure you're safe and sound out there."

"I'm sure you're right. I do have a big dog to protect me."

"Well, there you go."

By the time we pulled back into the library parking lot, the sun had set. The sky was an almost neon blue. The lot was empty but for Shirley's old little Toyota Corolla, silver, with doilies covering the back window shelf.

"You've been so generous, and so kind. Thank you," she said. "See you again, I hope. Please don't be shy. We're all neighbors out here, in the wilderness."

And with that, she got out and shut the door. I watched in the rearview mirror. She unlocked the car, got in, started it, and flashed her lights at me. I drove out of the lot, Shirley following, and back through Bethsmane, toward Levant. Who were these strange drugged people roaming around, blowing up trailer homes? Cooking what, exactly? Cooking? From the top of the hill, where Route 17 met Main Road, I could see the lights of the strip mall, where I knew there to be a McDonald's. I supposed I could go there, ask whether anyone working behind the counter had known Magda, if anyone might want her dead, and so forth. But that's what a police detective would do. I didn't want there to be any intrigue, any gossip. I'd been discreet enough with Shirley. I took out Blake's poem and held it in my hand as I drove. **They stumble all night over bones of the dead, And feel**

**they know not what but care, And wish to lead others, when they should be led.** Perhaps Blake was referring to those druggies, stumbling. Maybe they would lead me to the end of my story. Maybe they were holding Magda's body for ransom. Could they be out there on the island, waiting for me? Did Blake know? I had to see for myself, I decided. I dropped the poem in my lap. Magda's hairbrush poked me in the leg. I pulled it out and looked at the hair spun around the little spokes. Yes, long black hairs. Magda's hairs. I will find you, Magda, I said in my mindspace. I drove faster, turned onto my gravel road and rushed to park and nearly ran with my purse up the gravel to the cabin door, so dark now, so quiet, just the moon glowing low in the sky. I'd been gone longer than I'd planned. Hopefully Charlie hadn't done his business inside the cabin. It would stink. And I couldn't punish him for that. The door was locked, as I'd left it.

"Where are you, my love? My sweet boy? I'm so sorry. I know you were waiting.

Please forgive me, my pet. My good, good Charlie dog."

He did not appear. He was gone. I went back outside, stared out into the pine woods, then walked around the cabin and looked down at the lake. He could be anywhere by now, I realized, after so many hours without my watching. Someone with a key must have come and let him out.

## Six

For so many mornings, I'd risen with the pale sun shimmering on the lake, white and pink and yellow softness, still sinking into my dreams, and Charlie's, too. But that next morning, I woke up alone. I'd slept somehow, exhausted, with the aid of wine. I couldn't have gone out and looked for Charlie. It would have been too dangerous to go walking around at night when there were druggies on the loose. I kept thinking about what I'd said to Shirley. "When I lose something, I retrace my steps." But I couldn't do that with Charlie. That wouldn't help at all. So now I had two mysteries to solve, Magda's and Charlie's, and on top of it, I missed my dog. It was cold in the bed without him. I had eaten a bagel for dinner, feeling too guilty and too sad to eat the roasted chicken all alone. This was why I'd gone out and gotten a dog in the first place, the deadly quiet, the loneliness of the empty house in Monlith after Walter died. My emptiness, with Charlie gone, felt worse. Why hadn't he come home by now? The sun was up already. We had our morning walk to go on, our breakfast to eat, our lives to live. Was he that insulted? Had he thought I'd abandoned him in the cabin forever? I couldn't wonder too much about who had been in the cabin, who had held the door open, even encouraged Charlie to run out, shooing him, I bet, scaring him, warning him not to come back. "Vesta's dead! Now scram, you dumb mutt!" Ghod had done that. I hadn't allowed myself to think of it, but I thought of it now that the sun was up, and it infuriated me. I'd been violated. I'd been attacked. I must be on the right track, I thought, for Ghod to lash out at me this way. Revenge.

I got dressed. I didn't know quite what to do. I must have looked a bit mad, heaving, tearing up. I hadn't showered in several days by then. Usually that would have bothered me, but I didn't care. I was too upset. I really felt like a child without its mother all of a sudden. I wished there was someone I could call. Could I find Shirley? "My dog ran away," I'd sob.

"You poor thing. I'll come around after work and help you look for him. Did you leave some food out? He'll come straight back when he's hungry enough. He knows where home is."

But I had no phone, and involving Shirley would only complicate things. I could imagine the kind of laughter I'd get if I called the police.

"Crazy old lady, the old Girl Scout, her dog went missing," they'd say around the station.

"Wonder where he went."

"Dumb old mutt."

"Probably ran away. Who'd want to stick around with that old hag, that monster, that witch? Hansel and Gretel, is that the story? The crazy old hag who lived alone in the woods? Or am I thinking of Goldilocks? Whatever it is, she's a bitch, that's for sure."

Brutes, those cops were, talking about me that way. Didn't they know I'd been the wife of a scientist? Didn't they know I'd worn the most elegant silk blend dresses, gone to dinners at the university? The wife of a state senator had complimented me on my hairdo. They'd printed my picture in the paper a few times. I'd sung in a chorus at college. I'd studied Japanese calligraphy. I once saved a kitten that had crawled up into the wheel well of an old man's car. And what were those cops good for? Pulling people over for speeding? I pictured their mindspace crawling with headless rats, spewing blood, white flashing neck bones, severed heads gnawing at dead headless bodies. It made me sick to imagine their thoughts, those monsters. If Ghod laid a hand on my dog, I'd kill him. I wouldn't even let him beg for mercy. I'd just slit his thick, white throat.

I could imagine what Walter would say. He would be thinking it even now from his watery resting place. "You aren't strong enough for this, Vesta dear. Your nerves are too tender. You are like a little bird, you are a sparrow, and you're trying to be a hawk. You don't have that kind of spirit. You are just a little thing. Be your good self and twit about. Dance a little, sweep the floor. My sweet feathery girl, death is not for you." I'd polluted the lake now forever with Walter. I should have emptied him into the trash, carried him sealed up in the thick black plastic, and left him in the county dump, where I left all the garbage I didn't burn. Not that I made much trash. Besides the wrappings on things, the empty milk cartons, I tried my best to use the big compost bin I'd bought at the hardware store last summer. Charlie was always sniffing it. They said you couldn't compost meat, but chicken bones would be all right, I thought. Anyway, Charlie couldn't eat them. They turned to needles if he did. His throat would be torn. His guts would bleed. Oh God, I thought, grabbing my coat. Charlie could be hurt. He could have gotten hit by a car. He could have been eaten by a bear, or worse. Nothing would keep him from coming home, I imagined. Not unless he was maimed and trapped. Maybe a boulder fell on him, I thought. But there were no boulders in Levant. And then, grace, I imagined he'd fallen in love. I'd never neutered him. I had that to be grateful for. He could be out there, rapt in romance, procreating as he was always meant to. Soon he'd come back, proud and relaxed, and demand a new kind of respect. "You see, Vesta? I'm not a baby anymore. I am a proud papa. Just wait until you see my pups." That cheered me. That made me smile. But I wasn't sure of it. Given all that had happened over the last two days, I had to assume there'd been some foul play. Ghod had come. Ghod wanted to scare me, lead my search astray. He could be watching me now. Without Charlie to howl, I had no idea who might be out there in the pine woods.

I opened the front door. I whistled. I

called. I was scared to look for him, because if I didn't find him, it meant he was gone. And if I did find him, it might be his dead body I would find. Was it better to look or not to look? I debated, one foot out the door. It was another beautiful, clear morning on the lake, I could see through the windows. The island was there. I could pretend that nothing bad had happened. I could go on with my day, walk through the birch woods, have my breakfast. I could plant more seeds, listen to Pastor Jimmy, dance a little if a song came on. There was more to life than a dog to worry about. More than Magda, too. There was me to care for. I needed minding. I decided I wouldn't go hunting for Charlie that morning. I would stay put. I would think, and I would not think. The mindspace without Charlie was wild and panicked, but it was also half empty. There was more room for me to fill.

Perhaps there was a way, I thought, of figuring everything out from the safety of my own home. Maybe I didn't need to venture out, to investigate. Walter was always saying how the world was mostly theoretical, wasn't he? If a tree falls, does it really? How do you know for sure? You shouldn't believe your eyes. Oh, Walter. Was he really dead? I'd seen his dead body for but a few minutes. Could he have been faking all of that just to get rid of me? "I'll send you a sign," he'd said. I'd been begging him to agree to do that. "When you're dead, will you come back somehow? Please try. If you can, send me a sign that you are there. And if you can, stay with me. I'll be all alone. But will you promise? Promise to come and find me. Even if it's very hard. Won't you? Will you? Please?" And so he'd promised. And I'd seen him promise. But I hadn't believed. If I closed my eyes, I could be back in Monlith. I could be back on our honeymoon. I could be in college. I could be seventeen years old. I could almost taste the bitter rind of the oranges that grew on a tree outside our house growing up. You weren't supposed to eat them, but I would and they gave me stomachaches. Or had they? Had I grown up at all? Had time really gone by? What had happened to my life, I wondered. And with that, I put out my hand for Charlie to meet it with his silky head, but he did not. So I was crushed again. Things might be theoretical, that was true. I may be imagining it all, but it still hurt. It was still sad to lose someone you loved.

I turned on the radio and made a pot of coffee. It was Pastor Jimmy. He seemed to be on the air whenever I needed him. "And God said unto thee . . ." I went and washed my face. "Man's sin is his blindness." I brushed my hair with Magda's yellow brush. "The blessed are those . . ."

I poured myself a cup of coffee and took it to my table. My papers were stacked in a pile, and not as I thought I'd last left them the night before, scattered. But I'd been drinking wine. From my coat pocket I pulled out Blake's poem. The pen he'd used to mark the lines was blue ballpoint, the same as the note from the birch woods.

**How many have fallen there!**
**They stumble all night over**
**bones of the dead,**

**And feel they know not what
but care,
And wish to lead others, when
they should be led.**

I still didn't understand. I wished someone would come and lead me. Like a dog
on a leash, I guess. Drag me straight to
Magda's body. Then the mystery would be
solved. Charlie, I thought, might be in pursuit of the same goal. He might be standing guard over Magda right now. He might
have swum out to the island. I could picture him, sitting, guarding her body. All
day he'd sit, waiting for me to find them. I
missed him. My throat clamped in worry.

Magda was a grown woman—that's what
she was, really; at her age, she was young but
fully grown, fully developed. Her breasts
were heavy and, I imagined, beautiful. Her
figure had that kind of youthful fullness,
curvy but slim, as though she were floating in water and gravity had no grip on
her. She was like a naked nymph walking
across the surface of the lake. I could almost see her when I closed my eyes. I could

go anywhere with my eyes closed, to the moon if I wanted, listen to the deafening echo of silence as it spun through space. That is the sound of silence, isn't it? The sound of death? The sound of nonexistence? The friction of not being? Everyone on Earth had heard of death, from time to time. **How many have fallen there!** Others had lived and died before me.

Walter. After he died, I began to dread the discovery of any hints he might be sending me from the great beyond. I couldn't even tolerate the thought that he might actually still be there, watching me sob in our bed, in the shower. Watching me scrape the mold off the bread. I sat for hours watching my own drool dribble from my mouth. When the car came to bring me to the university chapel for the memorial, I wasn't even dressed. I put on an everyday outfit. I'd worn black my whole life. "Who are you?" Walter had asked when he met me. It was a setup. I dressed in black from day one. "Are you some kind of black widow?" I didn't have to change for death. It was always there. I'd been dressed for his funeral from the day we met. Those ashes. That urn. Walter was still in that lake out there. He hadn't really left, after all. I wished I hadn't asked him to stick around. His voice in my mindspace was still like a nosy adversary. Whenever I felt happy or sad, there he came, putting thoughts in my head, asking me to explain myself. I never should have married an academic. They always need to analyze and prove a point about something. Well, prove a point now, Walter, I said to the mindspace. Prove a point with Magda. If you're so smart. Did Ghod kill her? Where is she? What happened to her?

I looked out at the lake, brightening now with the bold colors of the trees around it. My little island looked sweet and peaceful. I would go out there. Soon, I told myself. But what would I do with Magda's dead body if I found it? Would I drag it into the rowboat and paddle back to shore? And then what? Would I bury it? I didn't think I had the physical strength to dig a hole big enough. I might have to hire someone.

I'd say I was burying my dog. Or I could cut Magda into pieces. Like the holes I had made in the garden, I'd dig and take little bits of Magda and place them in the black dirt, cover them up, sprinkle water from the can, watch through the kitchen window every morning as the sun shone down. I'd wait for Magda's roots to grow, a stalk to split through the earth and up into the warm, fizzling spring air. What would that plant look like? Would it bear fruit? Could I eat it? Would it kill me? Perhaps pieces of her were already buried out there. Something had been done in the garden. Why pluck out my seeds if you weren't going to plant something in their place? But if Magda didn't grow, that would be terrible. Meat was not compostable. Soon it would rot and start to stink. Charlie could dig up the garden and carry a severed hand into the cabin, bury it between the cushions of the couch. But he was gone. I missed him. I looked at Blake's poem again. **Bones of the dead.** Magda wasn't bones yet. Not unless her flesh had been pecked off by vultures. And I'd seen no vultures circling. She was still intact. She had to be. Could she still be alive?

And with that, it seemed silly to sit around being idle. I decided to be brave. I'd go out and look for Charlie. I'd put the effort in. If I found him dead, at least I'd know. I could get another dog. But it would never be the same. Charlie was my family. My throat clenched, and I choked and coughed as I put on my coat and got my purse and keys and shut the cabin door. I locked it. I didn't want anyone coming in, burying severed hands in my couch, or worse—burying severed hands in my couch, and then removing them, so that I'd never know. But I'd want to know if someone came and tried to bury hands. I'd never know, unless I left the door open. So I unlocked the door, and did what I'd seen done once on a television show. I got a spool of white thread, which I'd used months ago to sew the split edge of a down pillow when the feathers were coming out—I kept waking up with a mouth full of tiny goose feathers. I unraveled the spool until I had a length of string about a yard long. I tied one end to the foot of the table by the door, about an inch off the floor, and the other end to a tea cup. I looped the thread through the porcelain handle, and set it on the floor so that the thread was taut. If an intruder barged in, he'd snag his foot on the string, but not necessarily stumble. The cup would skid and chip against the wood-burning stove. Then I'd know. Even if the intruder set the cup back in its place, I'd see the cracks. I'd know the truth of what had happened. I closed the door gently behind me and went to the car, ready to drive around Levant with my window rolled down, calling out to Charlie. "Hey, boy. Hey, Charlie. Come out. Come out of the woods and down to the road." He'd hear me and come dashing, if he could. Soon we would be reunited, and we'd sleep the night curled up together under the covers. A cool breeze would blow. And I'd pet him and kiss him and promise never to leave him alone, not again, not for more than a second. And he'd purr and lick my face and groan and snuggle closer and we'd dream together. It would be so nice.

In the car, I put the key into the ignition and turned it. But nothing happened. The whole car felt dead. Not even a click or a kick came from the engine. I took the key out and tried again. It must be the battery, I thought. It must need a jump. Maybe I had left the lights on, or the door ajar. But what did I know about cars? It could be anything. If I had a phone, I could have called a tow truck, or even asked a mechanic to come give me an estimate right then and there. I could picture the man in his greasy gray overalls, smoking a cigarette and looking down at the lake. "Great place you have here. You know this used to be a Girl Scout camp?"

"Yes, I do know. Now, what about my car? Can you help me?"

"What you have here is a wiring issue. Looks like one of these wires has been severed."

"Severed, you say?"

"Cut, that means."

"I know what it means."

"Now, I'm just trying to help you out, ma'am. I didn't come all this way to get your goat."

"There's no goat, sir," I'd say. Oh, I'd be huffy. "Who cut the wire? What does that mean?"

"It means someone's come out and cut the wire. Now, maybe you cut it. How could I know who cut it?"

"Why would I cut my own wire? Do people do such things?"

"Lonely people do. Like when you call an ambulance because you've just slit your wrists."

"My goodness."

"You think you're the first?"

"I'm neither the first nor second. I'm none of those people. I haven't slit or severed a thing."

"Whatever you say. I'm just here to help you get your wires right."

"I'd appreciate it."

"I'm at your service, ma'am."

"Call me Vesta."

"All right, Vesta."

"And?"

"And what?"

"Can you fix it?"

"It can't be fixed. What you have here is irreparable damage. Don't you know there is no life after death? You know this is it, don't you? You aren't going anywhere."

"It can't be. I'll walk if I have to."

"You can try, Miss Vesta. But all I can say is that when you walk into that forest, that forest is all you'll see."

"Pastor Jimmy says—"

"Pastor Jimmy's been dead for years. Those radio shows? All reruns. All the same sput sputtered on and on. 'My husband has testicular cancer. Does that mean he's having an affair?'"

"How did you know about my husband?"

"Who wouldn't guess?"

"I couldn't have. I had no idea."

"How many have fallen here?" and he'd point to the red rock that jutted out by the water.

"How should I know?"

"You should know these things. Or are you a know-nothing? Have you not been educated?"

"You sound like my husband."

"He must have loved you."

"He's there now." I'd point out to the lake. And there'd come Charlie, splashing back in from the lake, a human arm or a whole leg dragging from his jaws.

I didn't look under the hood. I could have clanked and blown the dead leaves out from under, what have you. I knew it was useless. The thing was dead and fit to be buried. That old hunk of junk. I'd driven it from Monlith to Levant. Sent for all my boxes from the post office in Monlith, prepaid, one by one they came. The furniture was all from the charity shop at the church in Bethsmane.

I walked up the gravel drive and onto the road but did not cross it, and went past the slope that led to the birch woods. I didn't want any more clues from Blake. I'd had enough of Blake by now. He told me I'd needed to be led, but I felt I was strong enough to do the leading. I had Charlie's leash in my purse, and when I found him, I'd loop it on and keep it there, tie the loose end around my wrist like a handcuff. And with this leash, I thee wed, I thought. Just as meaningful, I'd say, as that ring that I'd taken off. It was now in a small glass jar, along with Charlie's baby teeth. I'd found them on the floor one day, canines, although it hadn't seemed Charlie had any teeth missing. One just assumes, though. And what do I know about canine dentistry? You see, I wasn't the kind of woman to ask questions. A good detective presumes more than she interrogates. I could presume that Charlie was alive, being held somewhere against his will. I could presume that Magda's killer was neither Blake nor Shirley nor Leonardo. I presumed the killer was likely Ghod. I did presume all that. And I presumed that my car had died by effect of my having driven it too much the other night. Something had been jangled loose. Or a small animal had crawled up into the works and nibbled through some wire. I presumed there'd been no intentional sabotage. And I presumed that by the end of this day, all my mysteries would be solved. I wouldn't be troubled by these matters much longer.

Because such things can't last too long without turning into major dramas. And this wasn't a major drama. It was a little cozy whodunit. A note, a lost dog, an urn of ashes dumped in a lake. I'd come up heads if I just kept going. Soon Magda would be recovering in the hospital, and I'd send her flowers and a teddy bear. It was probably all a gross misunderstanding.

I didn't know exactly where to walk, but I felt I ought to avoid the birch woods. Charlie wouldn't be there. The sight of those lovely trees, their soft whiteness blurred through the sunshine, chilled me. I walked up the main road and listed the remaining characters in my story. There was Henry. He had the strength and the bruised spirit to keep a dog tied up behind his store, perhaps as a favor he owed to Ghod. And he was also a kind of earthy, warm person whom Charlie might obey. The walk to Henry's store was about three miles. I could go there, act as though I needed to use the phone, poke around, jiggle the handles of any doors I found out back. Charlie might be in a basement, tied to an old hissing radiator. He might not have water. Oh, he would be so sad down there. I hoped Ghod or Henry hadn't been beating him, poor thing. As I walked along the road, I kept to the verge of dirt next to the crumbling edge of the gray paved road. It gleamed nearly white at certain points when I looked ahead of me.

I'd walked about a mile when I arrived at the turn in the road where the neighbors' drive opened up on the side, a clearing between the pines and a long, twisted lane of dirt. I stopped and stood, considering what I might find if I followed it. A weathered tin mailbox sat on a post at the shoulder. Nobody was watching, so I went and looked inside of it. The mail I pulled out was a coupon circular addressed to "Current Resident" and what looked to me like a hospital bill. I put the bill in my inside coat pocket and was about to continue down the main road, to get at a safe enough distance to tear it open and find out what I could find out about this neighbor's medical predicament. Maybe these were the charges for stitches to her hand from when she'd grappled with Magda and her switchblade. She may have been an accomplice to Ghod. If Ghod was extorting Magda, he could be extorting the neighbor as well. But tampering with the mail was a felony, wasn't it? I wasn't a criminal. I was above the law, yes, in that I was above Ghod. I was higher up on the scales of justice than the police. I couldn't tamper. I could only engage.

So I started up on the dirt lane through the pine trees, the echo of the day under the open sky immediately dulling and diminishing down inside the dark forest. Bit by bit I could feel my breathing get heavy, labored. I rested, wheezing. It was alarming how allergic I was to those pines. They were toxic to me, and yet I'd managed perfectly well for an entire year staying out of them in such close proximity. I continued on. I would persevere. I saw no paw prints, nor any footprints in the dirt, which was packed down by two running paths of tire marks, the treads like a city skyline. Funny what the imagination will fixate on when one's lungs are doing what, I don't know, filling with fluid? Clamping shut? Expanding like pancake batter when you add in the baking soda, frothing up? It was like breathing through a thin straw, the air sharp and stabbing in my chest. From the outside I probably looked like a feeble, worn-down old lady. By the time I reached the neighbors' gravel driveway, saw their big black car parked, their gray clapboard cabin—bigger than mine but no nicer—sitting there on the lake, I was seeing stars. I made my way to the clearing and stumbled across their lawn—they had grass there—and went and plunked myself down by the lake and waited, thinking almost nothing, and breathing, slowly, slowly, and eventually my lungs began to expand, my heart slowed, and I could inhale and exhale almost normally. By then two distinct forms had appeared to my right, shadows longer than seemed feasible considering the sun's position in the sky. One was the man and the other was the woman. They looked startled, and I must have as well. They were dressed up. They looked like they'd stepped out of some

old-timey postcard, the kind of photo-
graph you have made at a studio where
they dress you in costumes and place you
in front of backdrops of the Wild West or
something. I'd seen such pictures, but of
course Walter and I had never done anything like that.

"Can we help you?"

I didn't answer. I felt for a moment the
world tipped on its side. I put a hand out
into the grass but kept my eyes on the people. The woman, wearing a tight corseted
dress with heavy skirts, brown as mud,
took a step forward. She had a bonnet on.
The strap cut into the thin jowls dripping
at her throat. She was at once elegant and
rough in the antiquated getup. Her husband, I presumed, took her arm and pulled
her back.

"Are you lost?" the woman asked.

"This is private property," the man said.
"That's a private road. You saw the sign?"

Somehow I pushed myself up from the
ground. The world settled. It was brighter
in the grass now, gentler. A few butterflies
fluttered. The cabin was, as I noticed, not

so drab. There were shutters folded back from the windows painted a dark orange. There were tulips coming up in the mulch around the front steps. There was new, clear glass in the windows. Their view of the lake was better than mine. I could even see my little island from there. A canoe knocked against the pilings of a new wooden dock. This was a real life, here, a man and wife, I thought. I'd intruded.

"I'm so sorry," I said, my throat now opening. I was suddenly very embarrassed. "I got winded on the walk. This must seem so strange, an old lady coming to collapse on your lawn. I do apologize. I must have taken a wrong turn."

The costumed figures cocked their heads. The man's eyes shone through with sunlight. The light was twisting through the large boughs of pines that lined the yard. It was nice there. If it wasn't for the modern car in the drive, it could have been a colonial homestead. It could have been a museum, the kind where actors portray people from long ago, and you can stroll around and barge in on them churning the butter, or making lard soap, or roasting a lamb, or looming, or hammering hot steel.

"Can you walk?" the man said. He seemed anxious for me to be off their property.

"Oh yes, yes. I look frail, I know," I said, then paused. The hospital bill crinkled inside my coat pocket. "I'm fine, fine. I think I am allergic to those pines."

We were quiet then, the man impatient. The woman whispered something to him. He left, and went inside, the tails of his crumpled suit jacket flapping behind him.

"Do you need help finding your way back to the road?" the woman asked. She approached me now, walking slowly, fluidly, as though she were being pulled on wheels. My head spun a bit, watching her face enlarge.

"I should be all right," I told her. I began to pull the medical bill from my coat pocket, but I hesitated and stopped. "May I ask, are you dressed up for something?"

"I have cancer," she said.

"I'm sorry to hear that."

"We're having a little party, to celebrate me. Better now than when I'm gone. . . . I'm not doing chemo."

"I see."

"The Victorians were obsessed with death. It's the theme."

"The theme?"

"The theme of the party," she said. "We're making it a murder mystery party. My husband thought it would be fun. A little game, you know. Some of us like those kinds of things. Friends of mine," she said.

I didn't know what to say. The coincidence—that we were both engaged in a murder mystery—at first seemed like common ground rather than a conspiracy. I wasn't thinking straight. I thought to offer the neighbor my wisdom, everything I had learned since I had Asked Jeeves how to solve Magda's murder. But she was giving me an odd look, as though I was looking down on her. She stepped away.

"Do you live around here?" she asked somewhat coldly.

"I'm your neighbor," I said.

"In the next camp? The old Girl Scout camp?"

I nodded.

"I went there, when I was little. We meant to buy it, when it was for sale. But then I got sick. I grew up in Port Mary." Port Mary was the closest coastal town, where the state prison was. I'd driven past it once, all those spires and curlicued barbed-wire fences like a fortress, a castle, up in the mist around the harbor. "I remember canoeing back and forth to that little island. There was a ghost story people told around the campfire."

"Ghost story?" I said. I tried to laugh, but it came out as a cackle.

"Ghod told us your name once. What was it again? He'll be here later. We've cast him as the lead investigator with instructions to come dressed as Sherlock Holmes. But he'll probably show up in his uniform, as always."

"Those black leather gloves—" I began to say.

"Yes," she said. "Those. Mrs.—"

"Gool," I said, not to confuse things.

A cloud passed up in the sky somewhere, and the sunlight dimmed across the yard. A cold breeze made me shiver. The woman wrapped herself in a shawl, which I now saw was like a spider's web hanging from her shoulders.

"Could I trouble you," I asked meekly, "for a glass of water?"

She paused, a worried look on her face as she squinted up at those clear, nearly invisible windows facing the yard.

"I have a long way to walk," I went on. "I'm hunting my dog. Charlie. Have you seen him? I've been searching all day. And my car has trouble, so I've been on foot."

"You must be worried."

"Petrified, yes. He's my only—" and then I stopped.

"Well, yes, of course. Come in," she said, but eyed me suspiciously. She seemed to have some idea that it was untoward, rude to show up uninvited when she was throwing a party for her own death. She gestured, and I followed her through the grass up to the house through the shifting winds, walking slowly, as my balance, my sense of space and dimension were still somewhat blurred.

"If you don't mind," she said when we reached the door, and pointed at my boots, which were crusted in auburn-colored pine needles and muck and dead leaves. "I just did the floors. Guests will be here in an hour or so."

"Of course," I said, and as I bent over to loosen my boot, I must have fainted. The next thing I knew, I was coming to on a burnt-orange velveteen settee. In the clear light through the windows, sunshine reflecting off the lake made me wince. There was an old grand piano, a cascade of calla lilies across a dark polished coffee table, books and books, all clothbound, a whole library of shelves on the walls to either side. A record of Schubert piano sonatas was playing. It was like being transported back to another time, another country. "Where am I?" I asked myself, and put my hand out as though Charlie might be there to lick it. The room spun a bit, a scent of burning myrrh, some clanking from another room, and I dozed again, my arm flung out, and then someone was holding my wrist. Strong, cool fingers.

"She's fine," said a man's voice. When I looked up, there he was, white as a ghost in his strange white blouse. He replaced my wrist on the soft velveteen. "You'll be fine. Your pulse was weak when you fainted. But I think you have recovered. Take some Benadryl. Can you walk?"

"I don't know."

The woman held out two neon-pink pills.

"Please, Mrs. Gool. How do you feel?" the woman asked. "I brought you a plate of hors d'oeuvres. It's all I have, for the party, I'm afraid." I took the Benadryl and washed them down with the water in a glass on the table beside me. The woman pointed to a silver platter covered in tiny delicate morsels. A tiny quiche, a strand of asparagus wrapped in meat, a deviled egg, a croquette, a fleck of goat cheese tart. I recognized each of these from an outdated magazine I myself had in my bathroom, an issue of **The Gourmand.** I didn't want to look at the man again. My gut told me he was not to be trusted. He reminded me of a vampire. I could picture him mutilating a small animal. He seemed not to like me being there.

"You'll be all right," the woman said. I guess I must have looked a bit confused, my mouth hanging open, cringing, eyes widening at the look of them standing side by side again like some haunted antique portrait. **A Gentleman and His Wife.**

"I really fainted?" My voice was small, distant, as if it were coming from out in the pine woods, a faint echo from the poisoned beyond. The walls of the house were papered in a muted gray paisley pattern. Everything was so fine, so ornate. It was nothing like my cabin and my shabby secondhand furniture, my rough painted plank floors, the dark-paneled rooms, the creaks, the stains of what, I don't know, on the old couch. Was I in a dream? I closed my eyes and let my head roll toward the back of the settee. I listened to the gentleman and his wife whispering.

"What's she doing out here, anyway?"

"Looking for a dog."

"What kind of dog?"

The woman cleared her throat and raised her voice.

"What kind of dog did you say it was?"

"Was?" I said, almost sleeping.

"Your dog."

"He ran away," I murmured. "It's so unlike him." I pictured Charlie again, or at least I tried. I could barely recall the shape of his snout, the color of his fine fur. He was about as tall as my knees. I tried to summon the words to describe him, but merely said, "Big and brown."

"I'd worry about a dog on the loose. You know there are hunters in these parts."

"And wolves."

"Bears are coming out of hibernation. Anybody wandering the woods would be in peril, in the night," said the man.

My eyes fluttered open. I tried to lift myself up to sit. The silver platter of hors d'oeuvres sat in front of me on the coffee table. I reached for one, but just grasped at the thin air.

"Should we call an ambulance?"

The man grumbled something. "This

dog," he said, his tone like an inspector. "When did it run away?"

"Last night," I answered.

"I think I heard it."

I sat upright. My head began to clear.

"What's that?" I asked. "You heard my dog?"

"Last night, past midnight," the man said, wandering over to the piano. "I heard something rustling outside in the yard. Bigger than a raccoon. It woke me. Is he rabid?"

"Of course not," I said.

"It could have been anything," the woman said.

"But it could have been a dog," the man said. He sat on the piano bench, took one of his long, hairy white fingers and struck a high note. It rang out loudly, dissonant to the Schubert. I cringed.

"I'm sorry about your dog," the woman said. She seemed to want to brush off this concern. "Can you stand, Mrs. Gool?" I looked again at the strange bits of food she'd offered me. It seemed unwise to eat them. "Our guests should be coming soon. I'd offer you a bed to sleep in, but I'm afraid—"

"I'm sure she's fine," the man said. "Do you know your name?" he asked me derisively. "You know who's president?"

"Yes, yes, I'm fine. Please," I answered, waving my hand.

"How many fingers?" He held up two of those long, crooked things, kept his gaze lowered to his piano keys. "Not that there's anything so very terrible about amnesia. Like Henry. He seems to get along fine. Better even, than if he'd remembered," the man mumbled.

"Henry?"

"The man at the store. He was shot in the face, you know," the woman said.

"How awful," I said. "I suppose one would want to forget something like that."

"Brain damage," the man said, tapping his waxy black hair. "I've read somewhere that each time you lose consciousness, a part of the brain dies."

"I don't think that's true."

"Are you a doctor?" His voice was casual, false, patronizing.

"My husband was a doctor," I told him. "He's passed away, but he was one. I never heard him say that about losing consciousness. You mean to say that every time you fall asleep—"

"He's only teasing," the woman said.

"Only teasing," the man said.

"I'm sorry about your husband."

"Well, it was a long time ago," I began to say, and almost let it slip that I had dumped Walter's urn and ashes in the lake. But I didn't. It may be considered a crime to dispose of human remains without permission. The neighbors might have grounds to seek charges against me for pollution, and that is what I felt I'd done, in fact. I'd polluted the lake forever against me with Walter's mindspace. Now Walter had all of Lake David to swim around in.

"I have a self-help book here," the woman said, moving to the shelves and pulling one down. "**Death,** it's called. It's been very helpful to me." The man rose and puffed his chest, walked defiantly toward his wife, and snatched the book from her fingers.

"Take it," he said, and held it out. I couldn't look up at him. "Perhaps this will aid you, in your mourning. A husband, and now a dog. It must be difficult." His voice was cutting, as though he meant it to stab me in the heart. But it did not.

"How generous," I said, and held the book to my chest as though it might soothe me. I hated him. He reminded me of Walter, pointing to my weakness and offering only his great intellect, ideas to comfort me. I opened the book, words swirling before my eyes. The woman sighed. "I'm sure it will help," I said. "Anything would help now. Any clue." I shut the book. "I'd do anything to find my Charlie."

"Yes, you have a mystery to solve. And you can. It's more than a needle in a haystack, a dog in the woods. You will find him, Mrs. Gool." Perhaps I looked sad, since although she was impatient to escort me to the door, she said, "In solving a mystery, it's best to look at the clues. And then assemble them in a picture that makes the most sense. And then you can recreate the crime."

"Who said anything about a crime?" the man said angrily, playing a strange minor triad on the piano.

"Well, just hypothetically. In the murder mystery dinner party, before the killer is revealed, the inspector is supposed to re-enact the crime."

"I know all about that," I told her. "I'm familiar with mysteries."

She was trying to be helpful, but the husband was very irritated. Then, as though he could hear my thoughts, the man asked again, "Can you walk?"

I got up. "I think so," I said. "Did you see any digging? My Charlie likes to dig."

"We have done our own digging," the man said curtly. "If there's any other digging on our property, I'd ask for the holes to be filled."

"Of course," I said, gaining my balance again. You'd expect a gentleman to come let me lean on his arm, at least walk me to the door, see me off, but no. He stayed there fingering the high black and white keys of his piano, as though threatening to play something eerie and upsetting. The woman glanced down at the hors d'oeuvres. Out of politeness, I bent down and picked one up—a fragile shard of goat cheese tart. It had honey drizzled on top. I'd thought the goat cheese and honey was an odd combination when I saw the recipe in **The Gourmand.** But it was tasty. The woman handed me a cocktail napkin. The man played a high, creepy trill, which made both of us jump.

"I guess I should be going," I said.

"I'll keep an eye out for your dog," the man said. I wished he wouldn't. I didn't want him anywhere near my Charlie.

"Feel better, Mrs. Gool."

"Oh, I'll be fine. Just overheated, probably. It was nice to meet you," I lied. "And thank you again for the book."

"Have you called the police?" the woman asked. "The animal shelter? Fish and game? You could post signs up around town. At Henry's store, for example. Or go online. They say when a person goes missing, it's the first twenty-four hours after the disappearance that are the most critical, in the search."

"Yes, yes," I said hurriedly, suddenly embarrassed and despondent. "I should get to it." I tried to look happy as we walked down the hallway. I didn't understand the house. From the outside, it looked like a simple rustic structure. But on the inside, it was somehow palatial. Perhaps it was my twisted nerves, my eyes seeing things. We passed the open archway to the dining room. A long oblong table was spread with glossy china. Goblets and candelabras. From the kitchen I smelled a roast. If Charlie were around, he'd be howling, salivating into a puddle in front of the oven. "How lovely," I said. "Oh, and you. I hope you make a full recovery. Enjoy yourselves. And thank you for taking me in. I hope I didn't disturb you too much."

"Please," she said, shaking her head. "I only came home to enjoy my last days on Earth with my husband."

"Have a lovely time."

I left then, walking across the yard, past their black car, and up the dirt road through the pines, thrumming my fingers on the book still held against my chest. If I didn't have that tangible object to hold, I'd have felt that what had just transpired was only a dream. I'd hallucinated. Weren't there spores in the air that could cause that to happen? Each second had ticked by so deliberately. The sun had already passed its highest point and would now be on its descent toward the birch woods on the slope. My breath caught again, but not as bad this time. I took it slowly. Was the note about Magda just part of their death party game? It was the kind of thing Walter would have liked. "Games, all kinds, are to give stupid people some sense of control over reality. But they are not in control—not them, nor you or me, Vesta. It's a strange cruel universe we live in. In other dimensions, death may not exist at all." Walter would have charmed those neighbors, I was sure. He was drawn to kooks, he'd said. The two of them looked like they'd been trapped in a cellar for years, the crackled pasty-white makeup slathered over the woman's face, but not on her hands. She wouldn't want the makeup to get into the food, I supposed. Poor woman. She'd had some female difficulty, I intuited. Uterine cancer, maybe.

The taste of that goat cheese had stuck in my mouth, and as I breathed carefully through the pine woods, I spat occasionally, my mouth watering like a dog's. I was reminded momentarily of something that happened in Monlith with Charlie, still a young pup and rather silly, before we moved to Levant. I'd taken him to the local park. One could let a dog run around off leash, and I thought it would be good practice for Charlie to learn to socialize, and good exercise. He was so energetic, it was impossible to exhaust him when he was young. He'd zoom laps around the downstairs of that big old house, knocking over boxes as I packed things up, all of Walter's things, his books, his pens. An entire fortress of outdated reference books and long legal pads with only the first pages scrawled on. I sent it all to Goodwill. I'd asked the university if they would like his archives for the school library. But he'd already left them all his important papers. His secretary had the files at the office at school. At home, he was just keeping busy, just writing things down to amuse himself.

"This is Vesta," someone said at the dog park. "She was married to a famous German scientist!" That was how I was introduced.

"Well, he was an epistemologist, not a real scientist."

There was a whole pack of older ladies with big wolfish dogs in Monlith. I'd seen them walking together in town. It's where I'd initially gotten the idea to get Charlie.

"Our children are grown, they don't even visit. If they had grandchildren and lived nearby, maybe that would do it. But having a dog is a different kind of relationship. After a while, even if your husband lives a long time, things get dull, you know. No man can give the same comfort as a dog. People grow apart. But a dog will stick by you. A dog will never abandon you for some younger woman. A dog will never be cold and ignore you after a hard day. He will not think you look any less beautiful in this than that. Get one, Vesta," these women had told me. So I had.

At the park, Charlie took off, galloping around sloppily, wide-eyed and shy around the other dogs who were comfortable in their relationships. He went off into the maples and I just had a feeling he was up to no good. Maybe he would dig up some dead thing, unearth a bone a dog had buried decades ago, or come to me with a rotting squirrel, some headless bunny rabbit with a tire print across its back, teeming with maggots. But it was not a dead thing that Charlie was after that day. It was another dog's watery feces. He stuck his face right into it, then rolled around so that it covered his neck and chest. Almost immediately, he started gagging, thick drool flinging from his mouth as he shook with disgust. I stood back watching him in this insanity, feces and saliva mixing. He gagged and gagged. But he was so happy. When he looked up at me and saw my horror, he shrank against a tree as though suddenly aware of how unsanitary it all was.

Then he vomited a pile of kibble—each little pellet swollen and airy, I saw, steaming in the chilly Monlith morning. What was I supposed to do now? That was the last time I fed him "dog food." I was mortified. The women with their dogs were preening in the low sunshine, so happy, so pleased at how well their lives were going. And here was my little Charlie covered in diarrhea. I couldn't put him in the car. And I couldn't ask for help. How would they help me anyway? Bring a bucket of water? Oh, I couldn't stand their pitiful looks. When Walter died they came by with casseroles, flowers, acted like the country had lost a hero. They'd all probably had crushes on Walter. Those hussies. Those useless hens.

I slipped the leash back around Charlie's neck, careful not to touch the feces, but of course it got all over my hands and the legs of my trousers. We walked out of the park, leaving my car along the side of the road, careful not to be seen. It took two hours to walk all the way home, and then the garden hose wasn't working. There was nothing to water in the garden anyway. No amount of fertilizer or water could get anything to grow in that dry, dead dirt in Monlith. I had to open the kitchen window and pull the spray nozzle out from the sink and try to wash Charlie off that way. I squirted dishwashing detergent all over him. The pressure from the sink hose was laughable. It took an hour just to get the first layer of stuff out of his fur. Then I wrapped him in an old towel and carried him into the shower. I figured the shower was safer, less splashing around, and he couldn't try to jump out because there was a fiberglass door that I could fasten shut. So I removed my clothes, too, and we showered together for what must have been nearly an hour. I didn't think to wear rubber gloves, it didn't occur to me. I just shampooed him again and again, scrubbing with my fingers, then holding him down under the hot water, talking to him all the while. He seemed to understand that he was being punished, but I didn't think he was old enough to understand exactly how much he'd inconvenienced and humiliated me.

The women would ask where I'd been, what had happened. "We thought maybe you'd been kidnapped, since we saw your car. It was there when we all left, and we just didn't see you. Where'd you go? We nearly thought to call the police."

I walked all the way back at night, pulling Charlie with me, as punishment, really. I knew he was scared. I hadn't fed him. I refused to talk to him. That was how I used to punish Charlie—I turned quiet and cold. I had learned how cruel this was from Walter. Some nights he'd come home, and I'd have his dinner heated in the oven, and I'd have the lights in the den so lovely and comfortable, and I'd be reading on the couch, and he'd simply walk past, drop his coat on the back of the couch, nearly hitting me in the head. Not "Good evening, Vesta," or "How are you?" Nothing. Later, in bed, he'd groan and complain about a student or a colleague or some paper that was due, as though his work were so important and he was so put upon by the trivialities of life. He had no idea of the trivialities of life. Early on in our marriage, he had passed those all onto me. I don't think he'd been to a grocery store for thirty years by the time he died.

I took some deep breaths and slowed my pace. I could see the opening at the end of the little road through the pines. I drummed my fingers against the hard edge of the **Death** book they'd given me. It reminded me, the look and feel of it, the crisp bound corners covered in the dark blue cloth, of a book Walter had given me once, I think, just to shut me up. **The Comforts of Phenomenalism,** it was called. Every time I complained to him, he merely pointed out that reality was a perception, and that my perception was inherently flawed because I didn't have the same education as him.

"And whose fault is that?" I asked.

"It's certainly not mine. I'm just another pawn here, in the chess game of life." This was a metaphor he'd stolen from me and used to mock me with. I'd made the mistake once of comparing our life in Monlith to a chess game with an idiot, how long I was waiting for something to happen, some move, whether threatening or banal, just so I'd have something new to do.

I didn't read much of **The Comforts of Phenomenalism.** It depressed me to think about existential issues. It made me feel I was living in a dream and that although I was powerless over my mind, I was also dependent on it to conjure up all of my reality around me. When I didn't like what I saw, I blamed myself. "Conjure something better," I told myself. "Conjure a bed of roses, a million dollars, a cruise ship, old-time music, champagne, Walter as a young man again, and you young, too, dancing in the sunset, warm heavenly breezes lifting your feet from the deck, nothing to worry about, nothing to be ashamed of," and I'd close my eyes and open them to Walter's balding, waxy head on the pillow beside me. He was still handsome, but there was no romance left between us. I'd conjured that out of him, I supposed. Maybe I'd wanted too much, to be too comfortable. I could have run away, but those stories never ended well.

When I reached the edge of the pines, where the neighbor's gravel road opens onto Route 17, the sun was setting already. How was it possible? I'd barely investigated at all, and soon I would have to go back home. I didn't want to be wandering around Levant once night fell. It would be a very strange thing to see, some old woman in her dusty coat grasping **Death** in her hands and whistling into the forest. Ghod, on his way to the party, would surely stop to ask if I'd lost my mind. But Charlie was still out there. I didn't feel I could live with myself just turning back around and going home, so I decided to walk to the store, and see whether Henry was holding him hostage. I could call a taxi to take me home. I hadn't brought my purse, but I did have an emergency ten-dollar bill in the inside pocket of my coat. Or so I'd thought. When I checked, the pocket was empty. I hadn't taken the money out. Someone must have stolen it, along with the neighbor's medical bill, which was also missing. The man, I presumed. I could imagine him dragging me from the front yard into their sitting room, placing me faceup on the settee, feeling my pulse weak. He had placed his ear on my chest hoping or not hoping for a heartbeat. I wondered what else he had done while I was unconscious. With his hands on my body like that, he could have easily found his way into my pocket. My coat had been zipped when I'd sat down on their lawn. And it was unzipped when I awoke on the settee. He was a thief. He probably hoped to sabotage my hunt for Charlie, in cahoots with Ghod. Everyone was in cahoots. Even Shirley seemed to trust Ghod. "Call the police. They'll come out right away."

As I walked along in the quickly dwindling light up the road, no cars passed, and so I opened the book and read a paragraph at random.

Nobody knows your sorrows. It is best to keep it that way, as expressing sadness often invites pity. Sensitive women or young people often find pity consoling, and so they pervert their tearfulness into superficial melancholy in order to be further comforted. Some may become dependent on this superficial comfort, and will entangle themselves in darkness so that those around them will constantly try to "brighten" their spirits. Some call this "the depression." Make it a regular habit to deny sadness when someone asks how you are coping. When you publicize your lament, the dead feel you've cheapened their absence, as though you're taking advantage of their deaths to reap the attention you secretly wished for yourself while they were dying. When you mourn openly, the dead feel as though they've been murdered. If you must weep, do it in the bath, or in bed alone at night. Do not dedicate your sadness to anything but the dead. It is easy to confuse things, which is another reason to be discreet.

What nonsense, I thought. To do the opposite of what the book decreed, I decided to be miserable. I tried to summon tears from my eyes as I walked. The sky darkening above me helped. I first thought of everything that angered me—Walter's constant belittling, a lifetime of boredom in Monlith, my dashed dreams, my squandered passion, the abduction of my dog, the theft of my ten-dollar bill. That got me thrashing, mentally. And then I thought of my loneliness, my approaching death, how nobody knew me, how nobody cared. I thought of my parents, long dead, and how little love they'd given me. I thought of Walter, of his nauseatingly gentle caresses. Even when he meant to be tender, he was condescending and controlling. I'd never been loved properly. Nobody had ever said, "You are wonderful, even your bitterness and neurotic energy are wonderful. Even your suspiciousness, your rigidity, your graying, thinning, hair, your wrinkled thighs." I'd been young and beautiful once, and even then nobody had kissed me and said, "How young and beautiful you are," not unless they wanted something from me. And that was Walter. Always wanting something, some permission to be boastful, some permission to have power. I cried and cried, thinking of the love I could have had, had I never met that awful, deleterious, pompous man. I let tears drip from my eyes, my head bent toward the gravel, and as they splatted they made a little trail behind me. Maybe Charlie would pass by later and follow the trail. Poor Charlie. He was the only one on Earth who loved me, and even he had left. My head began to throb. I got dizzy again. The moon was up. The stars would come out. Ahead I could see the yellow lights of Henry's store, the single gas pump, the blur of pink neon from the sign that I knew read "Cold Beer."

Inside, Henry stood behind the counter with his back facing me, arranging cartons of cigarettes. I hid between the aisles of bread and cereal. It was a wonder a place like that could stay in business. I imagined the only people who went there regularly were the residents of Levant who

could not afford the gas to the strip mall
in Bethsmane. I'd seen such poor people
counting their change, drinking from two-
liter soda bottles in their trucks. I was indeed fortunate. The Girl Scout camp had
been so cheap. I thought of the poor people, how they weathered things with such
tough skins. They were the kind of people
who could swallow their sorrows, be brave,
be selfless, just as this **Death** book pre-
scribed. I paced the aisles of Henry's store,
my boots squeaking on the linoleum floors.
In the one refrigerator case there were just
three half-gallon jugs of milk, a couple of
packages of imitation cheese, butter, mar-
garine, and bacon, the kind that's presliced
and sealed in clear plastic. There was a
large neon orange "99 cents" sticker on it.
The store carried basic household goods—
sprays and cleaners, various hardware, big
boxes of matches, jars and cans of food,
and sundries. The shelving was aluminum
painted off-white, with little round holes
punched through. I slid **Death** under a
loaf of bread. I no longer wanted it. And
I didn't want to seem suspicious, walking

with such a book. That would look very
odd. "She must be out walking around,
lamenting the dead," Henry would think.
But I'm not so sure how much Henry did
think at all. The back of his head was
muddled on one side, long graying hairs
combed over what looked like mushy scar
tissue covered in skin white and thin in
spots, then blushing darkly into indigo. I
was a little nervous to speak to him. The
times I'd visited the store before, I'd had
Charlie with me to distract me from his
face. It was easy not to look him in the
eye then. But now it was just him and me,
the darkening evening outside. He'd said
nothing when I walked in. Maybe he had
hearing loss.

"Finding everything all right?" he asked
suddenly, without turning around. He
didn't sound like such an idiot. I worked
up the courage to walk up to the counter,
empty handed.

"This is very embarrassing," I said, looking down at the little rack of chewing gum
by the register. "But I seem to have left my
money at home, and I've been out looking

for my dog, and it's gotten too late to walk home, and there's a problem with my car, and I wonder, have you seen a dog come by?"

"It's not safe for a lady to be walking out alone at night," he said almost accusingly. I tried to look up into his face. It looked like his skull had been worn away on one side. I could see where the shotgun had blown part of his head off.

"I didn't intend to be walking around at night when I left the house," I said defensively. "So you haven't seen a dog around? Nothing strange?"

"Strange is relative," he said. He reached beneath the counter and brought out the phone, a black old-fashioned thing that looked greasy and marked up with fingerprints. "I haven't seen your dog," he told me, now reaching down under the counter again. This time he pulled out the slim phone book for the Bethsmane area. "You can look up the number for animal control. And Leo Smith. He's the only person I know works by giving rides. Pay me back for the calls next time you're in the store."

"May I ask you, sir, have you ever heard of a girl named Magda?"

"Mary Magdalene?" he thumbed his nose and sat down on a tall stool. "I didn't take you for a Christian."

"Oh, I'm not. I was just wondering—"

He scratched at the blown-off side of his head. He must have had awful headaches. I couldn't imagine what that would have felt like. I wanted to ask, but I was holding the receiver in my hand now. I flipped through the phone book and found Leo Smith's number. I dialed, smiling and nodding at the disfigured man. It was a miracle he'd survived. I wondered if he resented it, having been found and saved. Or had he saved himself? Stood up and held a towel to his head, brushed the shredded brains from his shoulder, and driven himself to the hospital? There were stories I'd read about things like that. The phone rang and rang, but nobody answered. I hung up.

"No answer."

"I can drive you," Henry said.

"Oh, I wouldn't dream of that," I said. And I backed away and up the aisles. "If my dog comes by, will you hold him?"

"I'm not sure I want to hold on to a stranger's dog."

"My name is Vesta. Vesta Gool."

"Vestibule?" The man chuckled to himself. "That can't be right." He shook his head.

I left the store. In case Henry suspected I was snooping, I made noise skidding in the loose gravel in the parking area out front, then stomped my boots on the pavement as I walked out of view of the store. Then I tiptoed back and snuck into the woods—just short pines, bushes mostly—and stepped as quietly as I could around to the back of the store. I could see light shining from a window facing the back, and a high chain-link fence around the back corner. I got closer, saw that the fence was padlocked shut. "Charlie?" I whispered. When I peered through the links of the fence, all I could see were cases of beer stacked along the outside wall of the store, and an overturned crate. The gravel around it was littered with cigarettes. I whistled softly. Charlie didn't bark or whimper. If he had heard me, he would have. He was not inside. I was relieved. I wouldn't have to fight Henry to get back my dog. But still, where was Charlie?

I made my way back to the road through the bush and jogged up Route 17, keeping to the center double line of fading white paint glowing in the moonlight. If I just kept to that line, I thought, I'd make it home safely. There was a distinct metallic tang in the air, and although the sky was clear I sensed a storm approaching. If Magda's body had been a real dead thing, it would soon be washed clean of evidence. If I'd believed in God, I'd have asked Him for a sign. "Show me what to do" is all I could think of sending up into the mind-space, which was like all of outer space above me on the road. One couldn't imagine how many stars were up there. I was afraid to look, afraid that the stars might spell out some answer from God, and then what would I do? If Walter had been alive, he'd pull up beside me in the car, insist I get in that instant. "Why are you being so silly, Vesta? Get in the car. There is no God up in the sky. There is no great conspiracy. This is what happens when you don't occupy yourself—you get bored. You start inventing things. Now, stop this nonsense. Come home and go to bed. You are exhausting yourself for no good reason."

"Oh, all right, Walter," I would have said. "You're right."

"You're chasing the white rabbit. Get in."

But what did Walter know about chasing anything? He made a living sitting still, just thinking things and writing them down, convincing others that what he thought and wrote was correct, and in this way, the world was supposed to change? His work was that powerful? I was sick of theory. What mattered was what a person did, not what they went around pontificating about!

"Let me see if I understand you. You say you are bored, and yet you have the entire world at your fingertips. You haven't even tried to use the computer I bought you."

That was the last argument we had, Walter and I, him convincing me to be happy and satisfied in the huge house in Monlith. I remember thinking, "I can't wait for you to die. I hope your tumor grows and grows. I hope that cancer kills you quick." And for weeks I thought of it there, in his testicles, a little pustule to start out with, festering with the rage that I was projecting into it. I channeled through the mindspace all the acid vitriol I'd ever felt for Walter, burrowing it into his body through the lungs every time he inhaled. That is really how I killed him. In my mind. I once heard Pastor Jimmy mention something called a "psychic death." Maybe that is what I'd brought on in Walter. Had it pained me to watch Walter suffer? Well, yes, of course, I had to concede that. It was awful. He was my husband, my one and only, the only man I'd ever loved. To watch him suffer was to suffer. It was excruciating to watch him die. And I did feel somewhat responsible. One of the first things I'd Asked Jeeves when I took the computer class was "What does cancer feel like?"

When I passed by the turn in the road, I heard no music, no twinkling crystal, no laughter from the neighbor's cottage. The lights from the cottage were dim but I could see them, glowing red through the thick of black trees. I thought to whistle for Charlie—maybe he was stuck in a hole somewhere out in the woods and would howl if he heard me—but I was scared to make any noise. I didn't want any trouble. And a part of me believed that Charlie wasn't out there. It was useless to look for him. He was gone, and I had to accept that. I cried as I walked. It felt good to feel so sad, to allow myself to grieve. I was haggard and tired and thirsty and hungry. I needed to be soothed, and there would be nobody to soothe me. And so I decided to soothe myself. I invented a new voice in my head: "Poor old Vesta." I could feel this other Vesta resonating in the mindspace. Perhaps the tang of storm was her, the coming of a new spirit into the atmosphere, replacing Walter.

I was very relieved to come upon my own mailbox by the side of the road. I rarely checked it, for I rarely received any mail. I found only a coupon circular when

I stuck my hand in now. There was an eerie quietude to the night as I walked this final stretch to the cabin, as though the trees were holding their breath as I passed. As the car and then the lake and cabin came into view, the sky cloudless despite the coming storm and lit by the full moon, which I finally looked up to acknowledge, I swore I heard a whisper, just a word, unintelligible, but just as sure as the wind in the trees was it the voice of a human girl, my Magda, no doubt. I could almost feel her eyes on me as I walked over the gravel and to the front door. Then I tripped on something on the path and fell face-first into my empty garden of dirt.

Suddenly the woods flooded with sounds. Crickets, the hum of life, everything at once—something was jogged loose in my ears. It was the kind of jolt one feels when one's heart is broken—the world becomes deafeningly loud. I'd discovered something about Walter a few months after he'd died. I'd found a little notebook among the papers and files and legal pads in his office at home, just a pocket-size thing, a quarter the size of the kind of paper Blake had used to write me that first note about Magda. Inside, Walter had scrawled out a list of girls, students at the university who had come to him for help, I supposed, and whom he preyed upon, listing everything about them that he coveted, staging mind games he could play with them to coax them into his arms and trousers. He wrote in German, his cursive hard, moody, exuberant as though his own writing excited him, flashy. **Mandy, long-limbed, tan, thinks I am a "genius with a cute accent." Likes animals. Tell her the story of the cat. Give her Schopenhauer, to confuse her, then preach.** And **Gretchen, short and stubby with big bosoms.** I used a German dictionary to translate. I read through each entry.

**Vicky**
**Joy**
**Theresa**
**Sarah**
**Wanda**
**Patricia**

**Clarice**
**Karen**
**Sofie**
**Jean**
**Emma**
**Catherine**
**Patty**
**Rosie**
**Amy**
**Rebecca**
**Joanne**

I threw the notebook in the trash, along with all his other papers, then wished, when the trash got picked up, that I had burned it all instead, had the nerve to burn the whole house down and scatter the chalky ashes in an open sewer grate somewhere, let all of Walter's thoughts seep into the urine and feces that must still exist somewhere in the bowels of this messy Earth.

Most of my erotic memories were from my adolescence, obsessive crushes on boys who reminded me of my father, spurts of mustache hairs, slight bulging muscles in the trousers. I always liked men with strong legs. And then one afternoon at a fair where there was a kissing booth to raise money for a community garden in the town where I'd grown up, I watched the eager young gentlemen hold their dollar bills and rub the BBQ sauce from their supple mouths as they approached the girls behind the makeshift counters. I didn't even look at the kissing, just the backs of those boys' heads, leaning, their shoulders cradling their desire like a baby they were carrying. Oh, I'd been deprived of so much by falling in love with my husband. I'd been so pretty once. And now I was ruined, an old lady with a mouth full of dirt. Enraged, I flipped myself over and looked up at the sky, catching my breath and then losing it again at the audacity of all those stars glittering above me, blinking and shimmering without shame. Even though so many had already burnt out, like me, they still glimmered. They still survived and hung there as though to say, "Remember me! I was beautiful! Let my light shine on without me! Never forget!" I was a coward for having lived as I did.

But never more, I resolved. I would persist despite my fear, despite my innocence, my depravity, my skillful denial of all that had pained me. Never again. After I'd settled in on the ground, warmed the dirt beneath me, let bugs crawl into my hair like Magda, I got myself standing, head reeling with hunger, and felt around for what it was that I had tripped over. It was a soft plastic package—my camouflage bodysuit, of course! I went inside, shocked to hear Wagner playing on the radio, and without thinking, walked directly into the trap I'd made, skittering the teacup across the floor and giving myself a near heart attack even before I flipped on the lights. I wiped the dirt off my face, undressed, and put on the darkness suit.

## Seven

I didn't bother to heat up my dinner. I didn't even bother to pour my wine into a glass, just sucked it straight from the bottle, and used my fingers to pick apart the cold, coagulated chicken, not caring that the gelatinous fat was clinging to my lips and gumming up my teeth. I stood at the sink and chewed and sucked and swallowed, staring down into the old porcelain, listening to the symphony, coffee grinds dotting a puddle of water sitting stagnant, reflecting up at me, black on white like the reverse of the night's sky. When I was done eating, I stood and breathed and collected myself. In the window I could see my face, wrinkled but gleaming. A sheen of sweat across my forehead made me look alive. When I turned the outside lights on, I could see the imprint of my body in the dirt. It was like an outline from a crime scene, my bootprints like marks to be measured and analyzed. I rubbed my eyes and when I looked out the window again, I saw Charlie. He was just sitting there, eyes two red beams focused on me through the window. I gasped and knocked on the glass, but he didn't move. He was like a statue, just staring at me. I couldn't believe it. At first I thought maybe he was stunned there, maybe he was frightened. I went outside in the darkness suit, breathing hard with anticipation, to see what condition he was in. Was he hurt? Was he frightened? I wanted him in my arms, to kiss his head and pet him and comfort him. He must be so frightened, having spent a night and a day out there all alone, doing God knows what, I thought. He stood now on four feet, backing up away from me toward the pine woods as I approached. Oh, Charlie, I said to myself. Do you not recognize your own mother?

"Charlie," I said aloud. I slapped at my knee to summon him toward me. To my shock, he lifted one side of his snout to show me a long canine, flared his nostrils. I stood straight and put my hands on my hips. What was this nonsense? I thought. He should be purring like a kitten to be back home. "Come here, this instant," I said. But I didn't get any closer. I didn't want to startle him and have him run away again, out into the woods. He stood stock still, straddling the earth like he was going to take off. I decided to take a different tack, and crouched down to the ground, made my voice sappy and soft. "Come here, boy," I said. He started to track back and forth, side to side along the perimeter of the dirt garden. "I'm not going to hurt you," I cooed. But of course I wasn't going to hurt him. Had he lost his mind? I tried to reconcile his anxiety and hostility by telling myself that he was just an animal, a slave to his instincts, and he was probably in shock still. He may be traumatized, but the moment he smelled me, I surmised, he would melt into his old self, be my pet again. Right now he was a wild wolf, afraid and on guard in the darkness. He must be hungry, it occurred to me. Spittle clung to his lips and flung onto his face as he shook his head **no.** I slowly backed away and went into the cabin to retrieve the chicken from the fridge. I darted around the kitchen quickly, but slowed my pace once I was outside. Charlie was acting so skittish. Every time I moved, he lurched to the side and roiled his mouth, flashing his fangs in the harsh white light of the flood lamps.

"Your chicken," I pronounced, bending down and setting the open Tupperware on the dirt like an offering. He was like a lion, the way he eyed me. He growled. It hurt my feelings deeply to be so distrusted, to be seen as a threat, unwanted, rejected. I went back inside and watched through the open doorway as he stopped and stared at the chicken, looking up at me now and then to make sure I wouldn't leap out and what—attack him? Minutes passed before he finally began to acquiesce. He tiptoed across the dirt to the Tupperware, lowered his head at last, then quickly snatched the chicken and darted back to where he'd seemed to deem it safe, at the edge of the garden, as though there were some force field there that I wouldn't dare to cross.

This is ridiculous, I thought, and although I was hurt and concerned, I was also overwhelmingly relieved. I hadn't lost him, after all. I stood and watched him hunker down with his cold chicken, holding the bone to the ground with his paws and chewing off the flesh. He looked playful from where I stood on the threshold of the cabin. I tried to relax and listen to the "Blue Danube" playing on the radio now. I would give Charlie his space, his time. Who knows what he'd seen out there? After years of domestic living, a night and day away were probably akin to me being picked up by an alien spaceship. But wouldn't that be worth the terror, to see beyond the earthly realm? Maybe he'd seen Magda out there.

I went inside for the rest of the wine and watched Charlie chewing his bone through the window, now smudged with chicken fat from when I banged on it with my greasy fist. When I finished the wine, I decided to open a new bottle. A bottle of red wine that I'd been saving for a special occasion. It was one of the things I'd brought with me, packed into the back of the car when I drove out from Monlith, a Mouton Rothschild from 1990, something Walter had bought and insisted we sit on for decades. "We shall drink it when something extraordinary happens," he'd said. And so it had sat on its side on a shelf in the basement along with other wines, which I donated to the Monlith soup kitchen before I'd moved away, not even thinking of how ridiculous that was, counting the bottles out in boxes, lining the back concrete wall of the church. The Bordeaux looked like blood in the dark-green glass bottle. I opened the drawer where I kept my corkscrew and found something there I'd never seen before. It was a black, vinyl-handled switchblade. "Magda," I thought to myself. She had left it for me.

It was heavier than I expected. I held it in my hand, looking for how to open it. All I had to do was squeeze at the metal edge, and the blade flipped up. The metal was cloudy, but the blade was sharp. Maybe it was one of those knives I'd seen advertised on late-night television in Monlith, the kind that can cut through pipe as well as slice a tomato without wrinkling the skin. I put the tip of the blade against the soft bed of my thumb, pricked it so that the blood welled up, just a speck of it. Yes, the knife was very sharp. I shut the blade. I was quite sure it was Magda's. She'd slide the knife in her back pocket whenever she went out, walking to work, or out here to the pine woods to meet with Ghod, to do his bidding so he wouldn't report her to the authorities. Why hadn't she just run away? Why did Magda have to die? Perhaps she'd told Ghod she was pregnant, to get out of some deal. She'd think Ghod would have lost his lust for her, but instead he killed her. It was a harsh, cruel world. Magda was right to carry a knife. Poor thing, she hadn't been quick enough to use it, crushed under the weight of Ghod's carnal fury. I'd never enjoyed it much, being suffocated like that, enduring what I could only tolerate while it pleased Walter so much, it seemed. He cried out in short whelps, always in German, my name called out not for me to hear it and know he loved me, but along with the fuck's and god's, like my name was some curse word, and he could shout it to marvel at his own erotic forbearance. "Wow, I am really good at this. I know, because I'm enjoying myself so much." That was what came across. But maybe Magda had a different experience. Maybe she'd been loved properly by Leo, and could refer back to that tenderness and attentiveness every time Ghod pressed himself against her. And inside her. I could imagine it.

Having eaten all the chicken, Charlie now worked to dig a hole in the garden of dirt to bury the bones. It seemed he might be out there all night, and I was tired. My legs twitched from all the walking I'd done, and my head swirled with the wine. I went up to bed, not turning off any lights, and left the front door wide open for Charlie for when he decided to come inside. Knowing he was alive, that he had returned to me, however suspiciously, was enough to arrest my anxieties. I lay down in bed, listening to the radio, drifting in and out of consciousness.

Pastor Jimmy was on the air.

"You've got to stop the anger in your family and restore the joy back to your life. And that will cause you to have godly children who will be raised to listen to the voice of God right away. They'll listen to God's voice. And they'll listen to you, their father. When I come home, we have dinner, we sit around the table and I say to my kids, 'What did God say to you today?' And they tell me. 'Well, I just heard God tell me this.' Or 'Today I heard in my heart God tell me this.' Or 'I heard God tell me this.' And they're hearing God's voice. And you know why? Because I've trained them to listen to my voice. I don't want God to have to tell them something a hundred times before they listen. I want them to hear God's voice and immediately respond. And how do I train them in that? By having them hear my voice, and immediately respond. I hope that you'll follow that policy and your life will be changed."

"Thank you, pastor," said a man over a crackly line.

"Now you have a good night, all right? Next caller."

"Yes, please," the voice sounded familiar. "What to do when you are angry for good reason?"

"I'm sorry now, what? Are you there, miss?"

"Yes, here I am." The girl's voice was raspy, and clearly foreign, heavily accented not like Walter's, but like Magda's. I listened carefully. I closed my eyes lying in bed, as though looking at anything would distract me from what I could hear.

"Well, say it again, dear. I didn't quite get you."

"Yes, please. What to do when a thing is not so good, and you are angry, but not that nothing is wrong. What to do when, yes, if there is something wrong and for good reason you have anger?"

"Let me see if I understand you correctly, miss—"

"Magda." Tears came to my eyes. The girl cleared her throat. "Magdalena Tanasković."

"Magdalena, you're called?"

"Mm-hmm."

"Magdalena, tell me if I've got you right. What you'd like to know is what to do when your anger is warranted. When there's a good reason, as you called it."

"Yes. Because I think some time it is right."

"Well, Magdalena, as I told the last caller, righteous anger is a sin."

"Yes, I know this. But if someone has hurting you?"

"First of all, I want you to know that the Bible says God will never allow us to go through more than we can handle. He knows us better than we know ourselves. You can make it through this, miss.

Philippians four, thirteen says 'I can do all things through Christ who strengthens me.' You are going to be fine. Now, God told Abraham, 'You are going to need to leave your relatives and go to the place that I call you to.'

"Not everyone has love in his heart. But you have to live by the Word of God, no matter what. And James one says 'Count it all joy when you encounter these trials.' It talks about being happy when people hurt you, when people are against you. Consider it a joy and privilege that you are, in a way, able to suffer for the name of Jesus by being abused.

"Now I'd say the number one reason women think their anger is justified is when there's been a betrayal by their husbands. And I'll say to you what I say to them. I say this over and over again. I cannot seem to say it enough. You need to remember that God has forgiven you for what you've done in the past. That's the most important thing to remember. You've betrayed God many times, haven't you, Magdalena?"

"I don't know. Maybe."

"Number two, people will disappoint you. You have to accept that fact: people will let you down. Sometimes we put people on such a high pedestal that they can't measure up to our expectations, and we then get disappointed. And then when they stumble, we get angry. Your closest friend could betray you, sure. Nobody's perfect. David said in the book of Psalms, 'If it would have been an enemy that betrayed me, then it would not have bothered me or hurt me. But it was you, my friend.'

"And number three, forgiveness is a decision. It's not a feeling. It's a choice you've got to make. You have to say, 'I forgive this person.' And you have to insist on forgiving them no matter what, even if you still feel angry and nothing has changed. And fourthly, you need to go to them and say, 'I forgive you. Even though you hurt my feelings, I forgive you. And I love you. And let's fix this. Those are the four steps that I would take.'"

"So if something hurt you, you say thank you, I forgive you?" Magda's voice was just as I'd always imagined it, sarcastic, cutting, and sweet. "You think, 'Forgive me and God say OK, no problem. She is slut anyway.' And so you—"

"You hear, folks, the pain of anger, how it cuts into the heart of the one who holds it, and spews poison onto anyone nearby? Let us pray."

I shuddered, as though an icy wind had blown across the room. I held Magda's knife in my fist, pressing nervously on the metal edge that would make the blade flash up. I would never forgive Walter. I would not apologize for his betrayal. If anyone gave me trouble, I would flash the blade. If anybody so much as gave me a dirty look, I would slice them. Pastor Jimmy ended his program with a short sermon on the dangers of giving in to the pleasures of the flesh.

I stopped listening when I heard Charlie walking around downstairs. He had finally come inside. I was woozy, and felt a little nauseated from both exhaustion, the wine, and the radio. I lifted myself off the bed and plodded down the stairs, first heavily, lazily, then tensing, remembering that the door was still open and Charlie might get alarmed and run out again. I tiptoed the rest of the way, hearing his heavy breathing from the lakeside room. It was the noise he made when he was irritated, like an old man. I walked quietly to the door and shut it. I turned off the radio, which now played some tweeky church music on an electric organ. I switched off the kitchen lights and walked lightly toward Charlie. He seemed to have curled up under the table, and as I approached, he lifted himself up and turned his back to me. It was so cruel, so cold. I felt awful. I wanted to be close to him, to patch things up between us. And I wanted to make sure that he hadn't been physically harmed in some way. Maybe he had scratches that needed cleaning, or even stitching. It must have been a horrific day in the wilds for him to be this closed off and angry at me. To add the stress of my neediness would have been selfish, I thought. So I didn't squat down and rub his head, the way I would have liked to, but I did bend over, just to try to see his face, his silvery head reflecting in the yellow lamplight, the wrinkles around his neck like they were when he was still a puppy, smooth as velvet. That is when I saw the shredded papers beneath him, like a nest. He'd ripped up all the papers that had been on my desk—the note from Blake, the poem, my writing, everything. It was like some kind of bird's nest he'd created, out of spite, I was sure. I'd ignored him in my pursuit of Magda, and this was his revenge. For a moment I wanted to hit him, but I would never. He'd even torn the blank pages from my notebook. I could see the twisted wire spiral and the hard cardboard cover lying like a dead thing by the leg of the chair. I lifted it carefully. I'd get rid of it, I thought, so as not to incite any more angst from Charlie if he ever saw it again. I was sad to have lost Blake's note. And as I carried the notebook to the trash, I opened it. There were a few ragged pages left, hanging by shreds.

On the back of one was something written in hard ballpoint pen and scratched
out. It was the beginning of something I
hadn't remembered writing. I turned on
the kitchen lights again and studied the
scratched-out words. If I held the paper
up to the window, darkness illuminating
it somehow, I could read the words. **Her
name was Magda,** it said. **She died and
there is nothing you can do about it. I
didn't**—and there it stopped. A false start,
it was. The only evidence left intact. But
how had it gotten there? I couldn't think.
I pulled the page out, picked off the shredded spiral shreds, and folded it up. Now I
felt that I had two sacred things: this paper
and the knife. They were charged with en-
ergies. I was armed now. Nothing could
hurt me. And yet I locked the door. Would
Charlie protect me, I wondered, now that
there'd been this rift between us? I imagined some madman breaking in, holding
a gun to my head, and Charlie just sitting there, yawning, clacking his gums as
though he were only disturbed that he'd

been woken up for the moment. He'd go back to his wild dog dreams. Ghod might be out there, looking in through the windows. He might have a hunting rifle aimed at me that very moment. If anybody was out there, Charlie would know. Animals had a sense of things. Walls did not limit their senses, as they do with human beings. A mere rodent scratching at a berry up the gravel drive would have caused Charlie to paw at the door, whine and yelp and cry until I let him out there to run around during the day. But now he was quiet. Too quiet, I thought. Silence like that felt unnatural. I put my fingers in my ears just to make sure I hadn't gone deaf. I could hear my heart beat on the inside, my own breath, slow and shallow.

I turned the kitchen light off again and looked out at the pine woods, into the dark. Something was out there. Somebody was watching me. I could feel it. I was sure. "Don't be silly, Vesta. You're imagining things," I tried to tell myself, but this was Walter's voice in my head.

I shook my head, blurring my vision,

to get the voice out of my head, and to see what, if anything, might appear to me if I looked at things a different way. I couldn't see anything, but the feeling of being watched persisted. I stared out, and spoke to Walter in my head. "I was half your age when we met, Walter. How could you think that was appropriate?"

"You were very willing, Vesta. I didn't pressure you at all."

"Did you think I didn't know about your dirty magazines?"

"Oh, please, Vesta. Men are men. We are wild animals. We have primal desires. If you weren't so frigid yourself, you'd have them, too. It's nothing to be ashamed about."

"I'm only ashamed that I ever let you touch me."

"I'm sorry, Vesta, that you aren't as beautiful as you like, but there is nothing to be ashamed of. You had a very attractive figure. And your mind, as well. You could have been a teacher if you'd wanted. Let me see your face," Walter demanded, a reflection in the dark window as his hand came to cup my chin, smelling of cigar smoke and aftershave. "Still lovely, Vesta. But let me see your eyes. You say you have no shame? Let me see that. Show me how big and brave you are."

I stared hard into the darkness. What would it take to prove that I was fearless, that I was strong, just as capable and smart and deserving as anybody? I felt the hair rise on my neck, as though someone were creeping up behind me, a ghost, an open hand, fingers outstretched to reach around my throat, grip, and strangle. Charlie growled, and I turned suddenly, gasping at the sight of him on four legs, head lowered, lips quivering, fangs showing, his eyes in the light glowing yellow like a sorcerer's skull, an evil lantern.

"Charlie?" I said, my voice smaller than ever. He heaved, staring up at me like a beast facing some interloper in his secret den, his archnemesis. I was some ignorant little creep whose very existence triggered furious violence. Drool dripped from his fangs, darkening the rug in tiny circles as his lip sputtered, his head trembling with rage. "Charlie, what is it?" He approached, his back muscles strained and tense, moving so slowly, the slow creep of a wolf hunting a stupid animal. I understood that there'd been nobody in the woods, no outside threat at all. The thing that had been watching me all along was Charlie.

I can't say what went through my mind in the moment he leapt up, his mouth stretching toward my neck, and my hand moved crosswise and down, away from me, a high-pitched squeak coming from my lips or Charlie's, but afterward, he scuttled backward, yelping loudly, and disappeared, leaving me in the kitchen standing covered in blood and Magda's knife gripped in my fist. It was the life in me that rose up, the desire to survive that made me do it, a gut reaction to kill the thing that would kill me. And in that, I was proud of my swift instincts. I saved my own life that night. Nobody else could have done it. I was alone, and so I was a hero. But now my poor Charlie had been stabbed. In my brilliant maneuver, I had slashed him not quite at the throat but somewhere along the chest bone. Perhaps my instincts had aimed the blade at his heart. The blood on my hands smelled bitter, like dirt. I tasted it, unthinkingly, after dropping the knife in the sink. Then I went to Charlie. It wasn't hard to find him, since he was crying the way he'd cried as a baby. Hysterical but rhythmical, as though the sound he made was work being done inside him. As I approached him under the table again, blood soaking the shreds of his paper nest, he startled and looked up, glared, shook his head, growled, and showed me his fangs like before. There would be no touching him, I realized. He would bleed to death under that table before he allowed me to come near. And even if I could reach him, hold him in my arms, examine the wounds I'd made—in self-defense, I knew this— what could I do for him? I wasn't a doctor. I had no way to stitch him up. I couldn't save him. I didn't even have a phone to call for help, or a car to take us to an animal hospital. I didn't even know where one was. I could walk back to Henry's store, I considered, call the police there, have them come and take him. But wouldn't they just "put him down"? No, I would have to make do alone. And as I bent to watch Charlie shake and rattle under the table, he seemed to breathe more slowly, to quiet himself, and then he closed his eyes. He curled up, shielding his chest from me. I could see his body rise and fall with each breath. The blood was creeping out from under him.

I cried solemnly, respectfully. "Goodbye, my sweet boy," I said. I felt no guilt or anger. It wasn't like when Walter left, holding my breath, desperate for time to stop, waiting for the lights to come on so I could see the way out. Charlie's death wasn't like that at all. It was soft. It was peaceful. "You were such a good dog," I told him, and finally reached out my hand to caress his silky head. Sometimes this happens to animals, I told myself. They turn mad on you.

I head into the pine woods in the darkness suit, concealing me between the darkening trees. Just try to find me, God, I whisper.

In my hands, I clutch a note I have written. **Her name was Vesta.** That was what I meant to write all along—my story, my last lines. My name was Vesta. I lived and died. Nobody will ever know me, just the way I've always liked it. As God approaches, I hold the note out. "Will you take this ticket and deliver me from evil?" I ask this with my teeth bared, a sarcastic grin. God takes the note from my hands and crumples it like it's nothing, like a receipt for a soda from a highway rest stop. "Don't be silly, Vesta," God says. "My little dove."

I run as fast as I can now. I feel the wind on my face. God follows but I get lost in the darkness. Maybe I can stay in these woods forever, I think. Already I can feel the poison air creeping in, clamping my throat shut, or perhaps this is the strength of my emotion. I can't breathe, but I run. Yes, yes, I will die out here. I'll do it my way. I'll have my say in how I return to the earth. The wind skittering between the thick boughs sways like a woman in a many-layered gown, moonlight glittering on her sequined lapels. She dances gently, but resolutely, in each passing breeze. When I feel myself slowing, I lie down in a soft bed of sodden leaves and watch the dance. The pines sway. My spirit lifts.

It is peaceful here, moving through the mindspace. Now I am a part of the darkness. I blend in perfectly.

# About the Author

**Ottessa Moshfegh** is a fiction writer from New England. **Eileen,** her first novel, was shortlisted for the National Book Critics Circle Award and the Man Booker Prize, and won the PEN/Hemingway Award for debut fiction. **My Year of Rest and Relaxation,** her second novel, was a **New York Times** bestseller. She is also the author of the short story collection **Homesick for Another World** and a novella, **McGlue.** She lives in southern California.